SIRENS AND SPIES

Collier Books
Macmillan Publishing Company
New York
Collier Macmillan Canada
Toronto
Maxwell Macmillan International Publishing Group
New York Oxford Singapore Sydney

First Collier Books edition 1990

Collier Books
Macmillan Publishing Company
866 Third Avenue, New York, NY 10022
Collier Macmillan Canada, Inc.
1200 Eglinton Avenue East
Suite 200
Don Mills, Ontario M3C 3N1

Printed in the United States of America
A hardcover edition of *Sirens and Spies* is available from Bradbury Press.
10 9 8 7 6 5 4 3 2 1

Library of Congress Cataloging-in-Publication Data

Lisle, Janet Taylor.
Sirens and spies / Janet Taylor Lisle.
p. cm.
Summary: No one agrees on the truth about the mysterious violin teacher, Renee Fitch, until she herself tells the definitive story of her life and brings together all the different views people have of her.
ISBN 0-02-044341-2
[1. Teachers—Fiction. 2. World War, 1939-1945—France—Fiction.]
I. Title.
PZ7.L6912Si 1990
[Fic]—dc20 90-185 CIP AC

SIRENS AND SPIES

1

Jimmy Dee came back to the house every night for a week after they took Miss Fitch to the hospital. He couldn't remember to stay away. Every night he came, forgetful and full of anticipation to hear her music, and every night he was surprised to find the windows black, the house shut up and empty.

Jimmy Dee had seen the ambulance come for Miss Fitch. He had heard the sirens and watched the police cars slide, pale and fishlike, up to the curb. From a hiding place across the road, he had watched the flashing lights, and he had seen them bring Miss Fitch out of the house on a little wheeled bed. She was tucked in as neatly as a baby. A bottle hung down over her head.

Right after that, Jimmy Dee had run away, going through back yards to the downtown streets. He knew as well as anybody where they had taken Miss Fitch. But, during the days, he simply forgot. As he wandered the town's frigid alleys or huddled in the nooks between buildings, the knowledge would pass out of his head. Then back he would come the next night all ready to watch and listen. It was winter, but he was used to being out in the cold.

Jimmy Dee first discovered the music on a rambling journey through town one night. He wasn't looking for anything in particular, unless it was a more comfortable corner to spend the night in. He heard the music, stopped and listened for a while and went away. But he was back again a few nights later, and again the night after that.

Eventually, his route took a pattern. His approach to the house never varied. Unsteadily he made his way along an overgrown hedge on the south side of Miss Fitch's yard. When he came to the open space of the frozen garden out back, he scuttled across, as best a big, bony man with too much drink in him could scuttle. He always went to the same clump of bushes. They were laurels, long and thin as he was. There was a fork in one branch that he had gotten used to leaning on. He could stay there without moving for a long time. It was one of the world's safe places. Even by day, it was unlikely that anyone, any neighbor for instance, would pick him out from that clump.

In the weeks before Miss Fitch had gone away, he had come sometimes in the late afternoons, too impatient to wait for cover of dark. No one had ever seen him. He came to listen to the music and to watch the wonderful woman who made it. He could see her clearly through the windows, bright and quick as a butterfly when she moved. She wore strange swooping dresses that fanned out like wings from her arms as she turned. She wasn't young, but she walked, he noticed, the way a movie star might, passing and re-passing the windows with her arms floated out and her head thrown back. Her hair was tied up in a miraculous puff on top. It fell down at the back and blew out over her forehead. One of the movements she made most often was an elaborate sweep with her hand that pushed the loose strands up and away from her eyes. She was, by far, the most exotic thing Jimmy Dee had ever seen.

But it was her music that had made him stay, leaning on the branch for hours in the cold. Now that she was gone, it was the music he missed most of all. She was a violin teacher. During the day, students came and went from the front of her house. Inside her living room they stood with instruments clamped against their chins while Miss Fitch drifted about them waving her hands. (He didn't call her Miss Fitch, didn't know that name. She was just lady, or woman, or beautiful.) Sometimes she played her own violin with her students. That was nice. The faint harmonies made Jimmy Dee's spine tingle, and if he had a bottle in his pocket then, he would take it out for a little drink to celebrate.

Most beautiful of all, though, was when Miss Fitch played by herself, later, after the students had gone home and she had made a quick supper in the kitchen. He had gotten to know her ways during those winter weeks of watching. She played to herself nearly every night after dinner. Jimmy Dee depended on it. He came if he could walk, if he wasn't so drunk that he forgot all about it.

Occasionally, she didn't play. She had visitors instead. A man came to dinner and stayed late. Weeks later, there was another, and later, another. Jimmy Dee learned that there was no music to be had on such nights. When a visitor came, he went quietly away knowing not to hope.

But sometimes, sometimes Miss Fitch sat alone in her living room and didn't play. For no reason that he could see, she read a book instead, or lay, motionless, on her dark couch. Then Jimmy Dee, standing out in the bushes, slowly froze with misery and frustration. He wanted to run to her back door and pound on it. "Come on, lady. I'm here! Play!" he would have yelled. He wanted to go inside and shake her into action.

He came mostly at night. The traffic noises from the town died down in the evening, so he could hear better. Then, the sound of Miss Fitch's violin came out through the windows and flew into Jimmy Dee like a warm beam of light. It fixed him to the fork in the branch. When Miss Fitch played alone, at night, Jimmy Dee stopped snuffling and he forgot to drink out of his bottle. Happiness swelled in him. It pushed back the cold, the dark, the rushing town all around and made a place for him, a little room that was his own. No one could say to Jimmy Dee while Miss Fitch played: "Get along there now!" No one could tell him to move on or get out. The music was his, all his. It was like something he'd found on the street, something special that had been dropped, left behind for him to snatch up and pocket before anyone else could recognize its value. Jimmy Dee hid himself while he listened in the same way that he would have hidden a pack of cigarettes he had found in the gutter, or a glove abandoned on a park bench. Where there was value there was danger that someone would snatch back.

But in the week since Miss Fitch had gone to the hospital, Jimmy Dee felt a new kind of danger. He felt it as soon as he saw, surprised all over again, the dark house. Suddenly he became more secretive about approaching it. Where before he had scuttled, he now slid, bent almost double, with sly, furtive movements. He paused often to look around, kept closer to the bushes, and though he arrived, out of habit, at the same forked branch, there was no safety there anymore.

Jimmy Dee knew, when he saw the house shut up that way, that they were looking for him. He did not want to remember why they were looking for him. He thought only: the music is gone; it is not safe here anymore. If some hand had reached out of the dark and grabbed him at that moment, if some voice had asked, "And where were you, Jimmy Dee, on the night of February 28, the night Miss Fitch sat all by herself in the room and wouldn't play and wouldn't play and

still wouldn't play? Now answer! Where were you?"
Jimmy Dee would have shrieked:

"No, I didn't! I ain't done nothing. She fell is all. I didn't mean to. I didn't want to. No! Leave me alone! I didn't!"

Night after night, Jimmy Dee slunk away from the dark house and, avoiding the street lights, crept back to the downtown streets to hide, and drink and forget all over again.

2

Elsie Potter said that she would not go to visit Miss Fitch in the hospital. Not only that but: "I wouldn't go if she got down on her hands and knees and begged," Elsie told her mother and her sister, Mary.

"She's in no condition to do that, the poor thing," Mrs. Potter pointed out to her daugther. On her face was a look she was famous for. Concern for helpless souls, Mary called it. Elsie said, "Weak chin."

"Well, if she could, I wouldn't go. The old fraud. She's probably faking this, too. She's always putting on a big production."

Elsie stood in the doorway to her room with her hands on her hips and her head held up stiff on her neck. It was her regal stance, the one that set her slight figure apart, more often than not these days, from others in a crowd; the one that so infuriated Mary. Elsie's hair was short and curled around her head like a dark crown. Her nose turned daintily up at the end. Elsie wasn't tall, not nearly so tall as Mary, but she had a way of looking down on people, a way of occupying higher ground which made height irrelevant.

"That's a horrible thing to say about a person who's lying half dead in the hospital!" cried Mary. "How can you say that? How?"

She was older than Elsie by a year, but softer. Mary would have gone in a flash. She would have gone on foot through freezing rain and blinding snow. She would have brought flowers and pretty notes telling Miss Fitch to get well soon. Mary had already imagined herself sitting on the hospital bed holding Miss Fitch's hand, comforting her, while Miss Fitch said:

"Mary. You are too good to me. I have been thinking of you, and look! Here you are!" Miss Fitch could make Mary feel happy about doing anything. She could make anyone feel happy. She was French and spoke the English language with emotional lisps and inversions.

"Ah! How you make me feel gay!" Miss Fitch would say, and instantly, magically, the room was filled with gaiety. Not that she couldn't be stern as well. Oh, yes, very stern, especially during lessons. But even that had its charm.

"For hard work there is no subsitute!" she would cry, striding up and down her living room, skirts flying, hair toppled over her forehead. And then turning, suddenly, to face an ill-prepared student: "But for today, enough! You cannot play today. Tomorrow, yes perhaps. We humans are not perfect creatures. Come. Listen. I will tell you a story about . . ."

She told the most wonderful stories. Mary and Elsie had both been her students. Once a week for over two years they had gone to her small home four blocks from theirs. They had practiced fingering, and tone, and management of the bow. And they had listened, rapt, while Miss Fitch told about the miraculous violinist Paganini, whose incomparable playing caused women to faint in their seats, caused grown men to weep. She would tell about Stradivarius, the great violin maker, such a genius, it was said, that he could hear in his head how a new violin would sound before its parts were assembled.

She told tragic stories of musicians who died, penniless, in grim garrets, who went mad on city streets while their children starved. She described the loneliness, the scorn, the illness endured by fiddlers long dead, and her own eyes brimmed as she spoke, as if she had witnessed these events and mourned personally. Then—up and out! She sent a student away shiny-eyed and determined, and welcomed the next with a sudden burst of arpeggio on her own luminous instrument.

"Soon! Soon!" Miss Fitch would cry. "Soon you will play this too!" Her students were dazzled.

"She makes me believe in myself!" Mary had exclaimed. "It doesn't matter whether I'm good or not. She makes me want to try for the moon!"

Only Elsie was unmoved.

"The moon is for astronauts," she said. "No one else could live there." She had not always felt this way about Miss Fitch. Elsie had been a believer too, and not so long ago. But now:

"She's a fraud," Elsie told Mary in the hall outside her room. "Always dressed up for the big performance and her makeup running in the cracks."

"But why?" asked Mary, staring, scandalized at Elsie's arrogant profile. "Why do you say things like that?"

Mary's face was the gentle kind that showed hurt easily. She was going to be a big woman, gently plump like her mother. Now she was just "fifteen and big for her age." In the hall, she stood beside her mother and their broad shoulders touched, and matched. Mary had her mother's straight, light brown hair. She had the same wide, flat hands. They were good hands, warm hands, and wholly unsuited for the slender neck of a violin.

Twenty-five years ago, Mrs. Potter had found out about those hands for herself, on a borrowed violin in the front parlor of her own mother's house. The heart was there but, after three years of lessons, the fingering was not. Mrs. Potter had forgotten her own frustration, or she had not looked at Mary's hands. Or, seeing the notice in the newspaper: "Renee Fitch, Concert Violinist. Lessons," she had simply jumped to replay history, to give it another chance.

Mrs. Potter enrolled Mary for lessons. Then, as an afterthought, she signed up Elsie, too. "So she won't feel left out," Mrs. Potter told Mr. Potter.

Elsie's hands were thin and quick, perfect extensions of her thin, quick body. ("Beautiful hands!" cried Miss Fitch.) The violin was her instrument. ("Made for you!" Miss Fitch gloated.) Mary's instrument might have been a trumpet, or a drum.

By the end of the first year of lessons, Elsie was mastering pieces by Mendelssohn and Mozart, while Miss Fitch stood beside her, swelled with pride. Mary, meanwhile, labored through a children's song book.

"She loves you," Mary had told Elsie at the end of the second year. "She can't help it. She's nice to me. She pretends she cares. But you're the one she really loves."

"I know," Elsie had said.

"She thinks you have special talent," said Mary, who was never stingy with compliments. "She thinks you're going somewhere."

"Maybe I am," Elsie had said then.

But suddenly, and for no good reason that Mary could see, Elsie had quit. She had placed those perfect hands on her hips, shaken her head and refused to go to her lessons.

"Don't ask me why," she had snapped, leaving Mary high and dry, and mortified.

Mary had been ashamed, at first, to appear at her own lessons. She felt presumptuous to be going on alone. But Miss Fitch was wonderful. If she was hurt, she never showed it, never once asked a "Why?" of her own. She had shrugged and laughed instead.

"She'll be back," Miss Fitch said gaily. "She has a gift."

But Elsie had not gone back. And now, four months later:

"You go see Miss Fitch," Elsie was telling Mary, with a mean shrug in the hall. "Go ahead. I don't care. She's your violin teacher."

Mary, however, was not the one who had been asked. Miss Fitch wanted Elsie, that was clear. She had sent a note to Mrs. Potter, who was holding it out to Elsie even now, as Mary stood aside in a fury.

"I called the hospital," Mrs. Potter said. She knew how to call a hospital and get results. She did it all the time for her own charity cases.

"They think she will recover completely if there are no complications."

"Was she . . . Well, you know," ventured Mary, blushing.

"Nothing of that sort," answered her mother. "Nothing carnal." It was her own inappropriate word. Elsie snorted.

"She has a bad cut on her head, from when she hit the table falling down. And one arm is broken. It was the cut that almost killed her. At her age, she went into shock," Mrs. Potter explained.

"Have they got who did it yet?" asked Mary with a shiver. "Who would do a thing like that to Miss Fitch, of all people?"

Mrs. Potter shook her head.

"Of all people, Miss Fitch is just the sort they would do it to," sniffed Elsie. "And that," she added, coming forward to peer at the note in her mother's hand, "is not her writing."

"Of course not. Someone wrote it for her. She couldn't hold a pen in the condition she's in," said Mrs. Potter.

"Hah!"

"Why you mean thing!" cried Mary, close to tears. Elsie looked at her, unrelenting.

At fourteen, Elsie had acquired somehow, from somewhere, all the icy composure of the high-school seniors who frightened Mary in the halls between classes. She was as cool and indifferent as they were. Elsie never cried about anything. Elsie never complained. Elsie said she would do a thing, and then did it, whether or not people agreed.

"I'm going out tonight," she'd tell her mother. And that was that. Out she went with barely a word of explanation.

"I think she has play practice," Mary would say, to cover for her. Or: "She went to the library to study." But did Elsie ever thank her? Certainly not.

"Say what you want, I don't care," she told Mary, as if loyalty, like charity, were a weakness, something a strong person could do without.

"But where *were* you?" Mary would ask. "There wasn't any play practice last night. I looked at the schedule."

"So, now you're a snoop, too," Elsie would answer, and Mary would turn away hurt.

This was not how other people's sisters acted, she'd noticed.

"Want to see what dress I'm wearing tonight?" Mary asked Elsie once. After all, Mary was older. She had dates now, and went to parties. She could tell Elsie about things she might need to know, things that other younger sisters were dying to know.

"No, thank you," Elsie replied. "What a waste of time," she said, and Mary, appearing from an afternoon of hair washing and primping and staring insecurely into the mirror, felt suddenly ridiculous.

"Why is she like that?" Mary had asked her mother. "Does she hate me?"

"Perhaps she's jealous."

"No, she's not. She really doesn't like parties. She likes being alone in her room."

"Yes," Mrs. Potter had mused. "I think she does."

In the hall, Mary watched as Elsie accepted at last the note offered by her mother, and bent to read it. She saw Elsie's eyes flicking over the words.

"She wants you to bring your violin," Mary couldn't help saying, angrily.

"So I see."

"That means she wants you to play for her."

"So what?"

"How *can* you play?" said Mary, bringing her hurt face up to look at Elsie's hard one. "You haven't played for four months, ever since you quit! You don't even have a violin anymore. You sold it, remember?"

Elsie's head shot up.

"If I'm not going, it doesn't matter what I did with my violin, does it?" she returned, cold as ice.

Elsie handed the note back to her mother. Then,

pirouetting on her heel like an outraged fairy-tale queen, she swept back into her room and rudely shut the door behind her.

Mary clenched her fists.

"Do you know that Elsie has never, in two years, invited anyone into that royal palace of hers?" Mary asked her mother. "Not even Heidi and Roo, her own little sisters. Not even Father. She makes him stand at the door to talk. Do you know that?"

But Mrs. Potter was plainly thinking of something else.

"Mary?" she said, as they walked together down the long hall, toward the stairs. "Mary? Why don't you go after all? Miss Fitch needs cheering up by somebody. I'll go too, if you like."

"But, we couldn't," gasped Mary, thunderstruck. "Don't you see? She asked Elsie specially. We couldn't possibly go. What would Miss Fitch think when she saw me and my violin instead?"

Mrs. Potter sighed. "Well, then," she said, folding up the note, "come downstairs and help me get Granny's tea together. I know it's Elsie's day, but . . ." She cast a helpless look at the closed door behind them.

3

But it was not Elsie's day. Inside her room, Elsie, after hearing her mother through the wall, veered to check the private calendar she kept posted on the back of her closet door. There she saw that Mrs. Potter had gotten it wrong, as usual. It was Heidi's day.

The girls took turns doing duty for Granny Colie, who lived housebound on the third floor. Although this schedule was meant to "help Mother get things done," it rarely worked. Like other attempts at organization in the Potter house, it floundered along from week to week in a sort of fog of disorder and forgetfulness.

"It's enough to drive a person crazy," Elsie told Mary. "As crazy as Granny Colie herself!"

"But Granny Colie isn't crazy," Mary had answered. "She's old, that's all. She's tired." The sisters could disagree on almost any subject that came up. They disagreed, for instance, about the Potter house itself.

"It's a lovely house," Mary could say. "I like living

all close together. That's what families are for, living close together."

"The rooms are too small," Elsie contended. "The walls are too thin."

"I like small rooms!" Mary would answer. But even she had to admit that the walls were thin, the level of noise sometimes distracting. Upstairs, the long hall carried voices back and forth like a stereo system. The Potter parents made rules in an attempt at privacy: no screaming (heaven forbid!), no loud talking (if humanly possible), and finally, no radio music after 8:30 P.M. Conveniently, the family record player had been broken for over a year.

"No radio music?" cried Mary and Elsie together.

"The little ones must have their sleep," Mrs. Potter explained apologetically. "That disco music gets them all stirred up."

"And I must have my sanity!" roared Mr. Potter, a sympathetic father usually, who only roared as a last resort.

"Mary plays that kind of music, not me," Elsie had said primly. "I play classical."

But Mr. Potter worked hard at his job. He was an exhausted man by the end of a day. Such men cannot always distinguish between kinds of music.

"Just a little peace?" he pleaded. "Not much to ask, is it? A little peace for an aging salesman?"

"And how about order?" demanded Elsie, who was cross about the radio curfew. "Order!" bellowed Elsie. It was her constant battle cry.

"This place looks like a flophouse!" she shouted. "A junk heap, a bargain basement, a nursery school for baboons!"

Well, perhaps it did, a little. (The little ones were insulted and went off to sulk. Baboons indeed!) Mrs. Potter ran a breezy ship, even on the best days. She was an easygoing woman who could let a layer of dust accumulate, could allow an appointment to slip past unnoticed, could forget to buy milk for two days in a row without coming unstrung.

"Mother does her best," Mary said. "There *are* a lot of us. And now with Granny so old and tired . . ."

"Schedules!" cried Elsie. "What we need are schedules around here."

"We have schedules," Mary said.

"But nobody writes them down!" cried Elsie. "Except me," she added. "I'm the only one who pays attention to order."

Even the little ones could see that there was some truth in this. Heidi was only just eight. Roo was six. They knew about Elsie's "order." Her strange habits stood out sharp and clear from the swarm, the hopeless clutter of their own world. Fascinated, they watched as Elsie performed the odd rite of ironing, straight out of the dryer, every article of her clean wash.

"Even her socks!" whispered Roo.

From around corners, they saw her polish her shoes, using a special polishing kit she kept under the sink in the bathroom. They watched her polish her wallet.

They saw her wash her hands afterward and scrub her nails with a special scrub brush she stored with the kit.

"Can I do that?" asked Roo.

"No," Elsie said. She dried the brush on a towel and put it in her pocket.

The little ones wanted to watch Elsie inside her room too. But Elsie's door was always closed.

"Can't we come in?" they chorused, knocking timidly.

"No."

"Please. Please. Just for a minute?" begged Heidi.

"No."

"What are you doing in there?"

"My homework."

"Roo's here. She wants to ask you something."

"Keep her away."

"But Elsie! You don't have to lock the door!"

"Yes, I do."

"Why?"

"Because it's my room and I don't want it contaminated."

Contaminated? The little ones looked at each other and shrugged.

"I think it means messed up, sort of," said Heidi.

Inside Elsie's stronghold of a room was another stronghold, equally mysterious, which the little ones had only glimpsed as Elsie passed in and out of her door. (The little ones dared not enter Elsie's room in her absence. "What if we are caught?" whispered Roo, fearfully.) The other stronghold was Elsie's desk, a plain, brown wooden thing that she had pushed into a corner, away from the windows.

Turning from the calendar, Elsie went across to it now, and sat down. The desk was scrupulously tidy, so well-organized that Elsie felt pleased just to look at it. Here nothing could ever be lost, or forgotten, or mistaken.

Elsie opened a drawer and pulled from it a blue spiral notebook, clean enough to have been bought yesterday. It hadn't been. The notebook was Elsie's private journal. She had been writing in it for a little over a year, and now it was almost filled. Elsie already had money put aside for another, and she knew what color it would be. Red. Her new notebook would be red and she would keep it in the drawer of her desk exactly on top of the blue one.

Elsie placed the notebook squarely on the desk. Then, sitting back to admire the effect, she respectfully reviewed, one by one, a number of other objects before her. These were the blotter upon which the notebook lay, its perfectly white surface secured at either end by two broad, gleaming bands of bronze; a gigantic, oblong pencil tray of the same shining bronze; a round box for stamps, bronze; a thick pen shot straight as an arrow into a heavy bronze base.

Traced into the metal of each object was an ornate design of leaves whose stems curled out in thin, elegant tendrils. The design swirled up the blotter's bands. It marched across the bottom of the pencil tray and lay atop the stamp box like a wreath. It cascaded down the sides of the pen holder.

The design was called Savannah Jungle. The desk set itself was barely a month old and amounted, in Elsie's eyes, to nothing short of perfection.

It was not, as Mr. Potter had pointed out, the sort of thing one would expect to see sitting on the desk of a young girl.

"Strange," he teased, when he examined the heavy pen. "Strange. I thought the Declaration of Independence had already been signed."

Elsie had scowled at him. The pen set was what she had wanted, what she had bought by herself, asking no one, with her violin money. In that way, the set was a declaration of independence all by itself.

"You sold your violin?" exclaimed Mrs. Potter, when Elsie had finally seen fit to tell her.

"Well, it was mine, wasn't it?"

"I guess so. Who bought it?"

"A lady. I advertized in the paper."

"You advertized in the *newspaper*?"

"Yes. It wasn't a very good violin, you know. I got a hundred and fifty dollars for it."

"Good heavens!" cried Mrs. Potter.

"And I bought this," said Elsie, taking the desk set, piece by piece, out of its box.

"What is it?"

"Savannah Jungle," Elsie had said proudly.

Mrs. Potter was horrified. She consulted her husband. ("She's an unusual child," he said, firmly, when he came back from looking at the set.)

She consulted Mary. ("How could I have known?" shrieked Mary. "Elsie never tells me anything!")

She had told even her own mother, Granny Colie, in desperation, over tea. That was no help. Granny Colie, who had given both girls their violins in the first place, two years ago, didn't like to be bothered with problems anymore.

"Which one is Elsie?" she asked innocently, stopping Mrs. Potter dead in her tracks.

"Oh, Mother. Don't be rude. You know perfectly well what I'm saying!"

Mrs. Potter had gone back to Elsie in the end.

"Are you sure?" she asked. "Are you absolutely sure?"

"Yes," Elsie had answered, without hesitation. She knew what was behind the question. Mrs. Potter was not disturbed by the desk set, or the money, or even the way the violin had been sold. What upset her was the act of selling, for it meant that Elsie was serious, that she had given up for good on violin lessons.

"And no wonder," thought Elsie now, sitting at her desk. She took the magnificent pen from its holder and flourished the point toward her journal.

"No wonder. The old fraud. A person like that isn't fit to teach anything. The witch. She got just what she deserved!"

4

The strange thing was that the Potters had seen Jimmy Dee not a month before Miss Fitch's "accident," as people on the street were nervously calling it.

They had seen him, but how were they to know about his visits to Miss Fitch? He looked to them all, all four girls at least, like another one of their mother's cases, which was bad enough to be sure.

For Mrs. Potter was a one-woman social-service organization. Everybody on Grove Street knew it. Everybody said it was fine, just fine, if she wanted to do things like that. Different strokes for different folks, they said, as long as she didn't turn her house into some kind of halfway center; as long as she kept it private.

"She brings them back from the bus station," said Mrs. Cornelle, who lived down at the end of the block.

"She gets them at the zoo when she takes the kids," said Mrs. Mott. She lived across the street and two houses up with a clear view of the disheveled Potter home. She'd been inside, too, once, courtesy of the United Way Fund Drive. A coat of paint was the least of what that house needed, Mrs. Mott could now report. Dust caked on tables, crayons grinding underfoot, wallpaper mercilessly peeled, a front stairway supporting ascending piles of mittens, notebooks, newspapers, stuffed animals, teacups, shoes.

"And there was Mrs. Potter in the middle of it all, actually smiling!" exclaimed Mrs. Mott. "And the children scrambling about, half-clothed, unwashed."

"Disgraceful," breathed Mrs. Cornelle.

"Pitiful," sighed Mrs. Cruikshank.

"The trouble with charity," declared Mrs. Landsbury, "is that it almost never begins at home."

The ladies met Thursdays for bridge and luncheon at Mrs. Mott's house, where their view of the Potter's home made it a frequent subject of conversation.

"I have heard," Mrs. Mott confided, lowering her cards with her voice, "I have heard that Mrs. Potter boards a derelict on the third floor. Perhaps more than one!"

"A derelict!" cried Mrs. Cornelle. "I heard it was a drug addict recently released."

"Whatever it is, it should be reported," Mrs. Cruikshank pointed out. "This is a nice neighborhood. It's up to us to keep the riffraff out, down the hill where they belong."

All the ladies nodded their heads. Yes, best to face reality. Millport was not the thriving center of southern Connecticut industry and trade it had been, fifty years ago. Over the years, factories had closed, businesses had moved, sidewalks had cracked and bars and questionable movie theaters had leapt like weeds into the breach.

Down the hill, fast food restaurants and discount stores vied for customers. Alleys collected glass and rubbish. Parks decayed, street lights broke, and clusters of seedy-looking men—of the type particularily alarming to women such as Mrs. Mott—could be seen lurking on corners near the railroad station.

Up the hill, on the other hand, Millport appeared in relative good order. The streets were largely residential and, while the homes were not fancy or very big, there was an air of respectability about them.

"Better than living in New York City," Mrs. Cruikshank liked to say. She'd come up on the New York train ten years ago to visit her sister, and she hadn't gone back.

"We've got real trees here in Millport and a downtown that keeps to itself, if you let it," she told the ladies. "Down there in New York you've got to hide your purse under your coat just to go to the market."

Mrs. Potter had come from New York City, too, years before Mrs. Cruikshank's husband died and set her up free and clear to live where she pleased. Long-term residence didn't get Mrs. Potter off the hook, though.

"I heard she was a welfare worker in the Bronx," murmured Mrs. Mott.

"*I* heard she counseled criminals on Staten Island," said Mrs. Landsbury.

"That accounts for it," Mrs. Cruikshank announced. "That accounts for everything!"

It was Mrs. Potter, of course, who had seen Jimmy Dee first. She was standing at her kitchen window looking out at all the snow and ice and more predicted. The afternoon was a dark one, late in January. She wiped her hands on a paper towel and he slouched into view, a big man, stumbling, going down the very middle of the street, not even watching for cars. Watching his feet.

He was cold in his thin coat, probably didn't know how cold he was or how he shook all over so that he couldn't walk in a straight line but chattered along with small lurches and weavings.

Mrs. Potter was out the door in a second to get him, with only her sweater on.

"Lady," he said. "Don't bother me. I'm going somewheres." But when he felt the heat from the kitchen, staggered into it off the back porch ("Don't push!" he growled at her), when he got inside, he collapsed down in a chair in a grateful way. Or his body did. He wasn't grateful. He was dirty and cold, shaking like a house dog left out on a winter night. He didn't want anything, not anyone to help. But he took a bowl of soup. And would she please quit looking at him and get those children away?

By this time, all four girls had arrived, having heard the rumpus at the back door. They stood like a small church choir in the kitchen entry, Mary blushing for her mother while Elsie said fiercely, "What *is* this?" The little ones were backed up against her.

Mrs. Potter said, "Elsie, will you run and get that bottle of whiskey in the cabinet?"

"I will not," answered Elsie, tossing her head. But Mary went and brought it back. Mrs. Potter poured a dose straight into his soup, and poured more soup in on top.

"You'll feel better in a minute," she said.

Next Heidi yelled: "Here comes Granny Colie!" and in she shuffled on the scrappy remains of her bedroom slippers. She was all the way down from upstairs for her tea, and breathing hard. The girls stood aside with blank faces, as if to let her see what Mother had done now.

"Who's there?" barked Granny, stopping short. She still had a sense for atmospheres.

Elsie answered coldly, "A man."

"A man? What man?"

Mary cut in to stop that. "I'll help you get your tea, Granny," she said, and edged her past the chair he was sitting in.

If he knew he was blocking traffic, he didn't look up, didn't try to make room for a half-blind old woman. He never once looked thankful that he was there. Elsie expected something, at least. She stood by in a fury while he slurped his soup. His mouth was so cold he couldn't drink it nicely. It spilled out all over his chin, catching up on the bristles.

Mrs. Potter leaned over him, would have touched him if he hadn't sent a warning through his eyes. She asked him to stay a bit and warm himself up. She said he could take a rest upstairs if he wanted.

"On whose bed?" snorted Elsie to Mary, who was attending to Granny Colie as if her life depended on it.

"Here's your tea, Granny. Shall I help you carry it up?"

Now Granny looked as if she didn't want it. She was feeling for lint on her sweater and picking it off with little flicks. Mary stepped in front of her in case he was watching. Granny Colie could pick lint for hours.

He finished his soup at that moment with a bang on the bowl that made everyone jump. Then he lifted his big, skinny body from the chair. His greasy coat swung down to his knees. He made for the door, head down. Mary backed Granny Colie out of the way.

"Do stay!" cried Mrs. Potter, going after him. "It's not any trouble. Just to warm yourself."

He said: "Are you kidding, lady? I didn't want to come in here in the first place," and slammed the door in her face going out.

Mrs. Potter went and got his empty bowl. She brought it to the sink, where she could watch him through the window. Then, perhaps because they were, Granny and all, still standing there staring at her, she felt called upon to speak for him.

"He was embarrassed to be seen like that," she told them. Elsie's mouth dropped open with scorn.

"He wanted to stay, but he was embarrassed," said Mrs. Potter.

"Embarrassed!" cried Elsie. "He was not embarrassed. He's forgotten how to be that a long time ago. He was a drunkard who didn't want help from any woman who flies out of her house to grab him. He wanted the whole bottle, not something in his soup. I'm surprised he didn't hit you up for money."

"He did," Mrs. Potter admitted. "That's how I got him to come in."

"That's crazy!" yelled Elsie. The little ones watched her with guarded eyes. "It was crazy to bring him in here. He could have been a killer and murdered us all! He could have been on drugs, not liquor. Why do you always do things like this?"

"He wasn't dangerous," Mrs. Potter said gently. "I saw it in his eyes. He's a poor, sensitive man who's down on his luck. He needed help. Anyone could see that."

"And you didn't help him," Elsie went on. "You can't help people like him. Even he knew that. Everyone knows it. Nobody else tries to bring creeps like that into their houses for their own children to look at. Even Mary thinks it's stupid!"

This was a challenge that hurt Mary more than anyone. It gave her the look of having gone behind her mother's back when it was only that she tried so hard to please them all.

The little ones put their eyes severely on Mary. She

stared. red faced, at Granny Colie, who was peering at something in midair that might have been her teacup if Mary hadn't had a stranglehold on it two feet below.

"Where's my tea?" whimpered Granny. "Where did you hide my tea?"

"Oh, hush," Elsie snapped. "It's right in front of your nose." Then, she bit her lip.

"Mother," whispered Mary, in agony. But Elsie wasn't finished yet.

"You don't think about us when you see those people, do you?" she continued. "You don't think how we hate standing there on the sidewalk while you talk to them, those awful people with stumps that sell pencils, those disgusting men sleeping down in the train station, those women wandering like zombies around the park. You don't think how it feels riding home in the car with them, not saying a word because they might throw up or have hysterics. Or pull a knife, some of them."

"No one has ever pulled a knife," Mrs. Potter said softly. "They don't do that." Elsie wasn't listening.

"Do you know how much I hate to go anywhere with you?" she asked. "I'm praying the whole time you won't see them, praying like mad they won't be there. And meanwhile, you know what you're doing? You're actually looking for them. It isn't good enough for you to run into them. You've got to look in all the right places to see where they might be hiding, to drag them out by their necks!"

"Elsie!" said Mrs. Potter. "Elsie, it isn't that way."

"It *is* that way," Elsie said, "and everybody on this street knows it. Everyone knows about the Potters' deadbeats. They watch us, and say things. Can you imagine what they say? Can you?"

Then she turned and swept out of the kitchen, pushing the little ones away.

All the time Elsie talked, Mrs. Potter had kept half an eye on the street. When Elsie had gone, she turned and faced the window. The man was far down the block by now, a gray shape lurching past hedges. Mrs. Potter put her head close to the window to keep him in sight.

"He is walking on the sidewalk," she reported to those waiting behind her in the kitchen. "He's still on it. There he goes around the corner. He is definitely on the sidewalk!" called Mrs. Potter.

"And bless the poor soul," remarked Granny Colie, so unexpectedly that they all swung around to look at her.

5

For three days, Miss Fitch's hospital note drifted about the Potter house unanswered. It sat on the hall table beside Mrs. Potter's beaten, brown handbag until Mr. Potter picked it up with the mail and asked, "Whose is this?"

Then it was cleared to the kitchen counter under the pencil sharpener, where anyone in the house with a worn down stub could read it again. It hung for a while on the bulletin board by the kitchen telephone, fell off into a pile of old bills on the shelf below, appeared magnetized for a day to the front of the refrigerator. From there, it vanished completely during an evening, and suddenly popped up again on the kitchen counter, just in time for Elsie's announcement at the breakfast table on the morning of the fourth day.

"I will go see Miss Fitch this afternoon, after school," Elsie proclaimed, just as if—with her nose in the air—she really were queen of something.

"Good!" Mrs. Potter said brightly.

"Why now, after all this time?" demanded Mary.

"I'll call the hospital this morning," Mrs. Potter added. She glanced at Mary with a question ready on her lips.

But Mary shook her head: No. She wouldn't go. Not without Elsie and now certainly not with her. Her forehead was knitted. She frowned at her orange juice and up at the kitchen clock. She did not look at Elsie, who was reading a history book at the table and not looking at anyone, either.

"You've done this just to be mean, haven't you?" Mary said, still not looking. "Mean to me and mean to Miss Fitch. You've taken care of both of us all in one swoop."

"Untrue," answered Elsie. "You don't understand the least thing about it."

"Oh, I understand!" Mary declared. "I understand how you didn't have a friend in this world until Miss Fitch took you on."

"She did not ever take me on!" snapped Elsie.

"I understand how you couldn't have a friend because nobody could stand you, because you were too stuck up to even talk to anyone. And then Miss Fitch made you into somebody special."

"She did not!" hissed Elsie. "It was all a fraud."

"And she cared about you more than she cared about anyone. She was different around you. I saw it. I saw the whole thing," said Mary, bitterly.

"Hush, Mary!" cried Mrs. Potter. Elsie had risen from her chair. She was gathering her books, preparing to leave.

"And then," said Mary, "when you saw you had her,

you turned against her. Suddenly she wasn't good enough for you. Oh, yes," called Mary, as Elsie walked stiff shouldered out of the kitchen. "I understand! Nobody is good enough for you, are they? Especially not the people who happen to like you. Especially not them!"

But the front door banged and Elsie was gone.

"Mary, I'm surprised at you," exclaimed Mrs. Potter. "That wasn't like you at all!"

That afternoon, Mary walked a long route home from school. She didn't want to run into Elsie. She wanted her gone—out of sight, out of mind. Mary walked twenty minutes in an out-of-the-way direction. (She checked her watch.) Then she walked twenty minutes back again. This should have been long enough for anyone to come home, comb her hair, check a bus schedule and leave for a hospital visit.

But time in the Potter house had a way of losing its grip. Complications arose. Plans dissolved and re-formed. So the first thing that Mary saw when she opened the front door was Elsie, lounging against the hall banister.

"I thought you'd be gone, by now," muttered Mary, just to let her sister know the meeting wasn't her idea.

"Actually, we were waiting for you," Elsie answered, half a smile on her lips.

"For me!"

"Heidi and Roo need a sitter. Mother is coming, too," Elsie said. "If she can ever pull herself together."

From upstairs came the thumps and bumps of a body in frantic motion. Mrs. Potter appeared on the landing overhead, then disappeared again.

"Where is my purse? Where are my gloves?" they heard her wail from far-off corners of the house.

Elsie nodded at Mary, and shifted her weight away from the banister.

"It's amazing we ever get out of this house at all," she said, examining her nails. She turned her arm over to look at her watch.

"You look nervous," Mary told her. "Is that why you're taking Mother?"

"I'm not nervous at all," Elsie answered. "Mother wants to go. She's desperate to go. You know what she's like with wounded birds. She can't keep her hands off them."

"You look nervous, all right."

"Quit that, will you?" snapped Elsie. They stood together waiting at the bottom of the stairs.

"What about the violin?" asked Mary suddenly. "She wanted you to bring it."

Elsie shrugged.

"Well, there's still mine," Mary offered. She hated to think of Miss Fitch being disappointed.

"No!" said Elsie, so sharply that Mary stepped away from her and went into the kitchen to hide her anger.

Then Mrs. Potter came downstairs in a great fluster and they were off.

“Heidi and Roo are upstairs playing,” called Mrs. Potter from the back porch. “And Granny . . .”

“Needs her tea,” Mary called back.

“Yes.” They got into the car and drove away. The house turned quiet.

Mary made Granny her tea and brought it up on a tray. But Granny was far-off somewhere in her mind, her head thrown back against the chair cushions. Mary left the tea and went to check on the little ones. They were playing with dolls in the attic, a dusty, unfinished room down the hall from Granny’s quarters.

Did we ever play here? Mary wondered, thinking of Elsie. It looked so cozy and private. The little ones knelt together in a dim corner, pulling pieces of material from a trunk. Their dolls lay about them, swathed in other fabrics.

“May I come in?” Mary was about to ask—for it seemed the sort of scene one should ask permission to enter—when her shape at the door caught the little ones’ eyes and their faces flicked up, pale and secretive.

“I’m downstairs, if you need me,” Mary told them instead, and she stepped almost guiltily away from the door.

Going down the stairs, she recalled a game that she and Elsie had liked to play together when they were little, and still shared a bedroom. The game involved transforming their room into a huge doll palace with silk scarves borrowed from their mother’s top bureau drawer. Each scarf, spread out square on the floor, became a room in the palace, and upon it they arranged such doll furniture as they had, and other things, like an upside-down tissue box for a mansion-size dining-room table, or a round piece of tin foil for a silver swimming pool. The palace might have gone on forever, for as many silk scarves as they could find. But their bedroom was not large, and—filled as it was with two bureaus, two beds, two toy chests—in the end Mary and Elsie always ran out of space. Then:

"It's too small in here!" Elsie would cry in frustration. "There's never enough room!"

In later years, this was a charge she had brought against Mary as well: "You take up too much room!"

Mary frowned, remembering. She sat in the living room on a chair by the window where she could watch for her mother's return.

"But it wasn't me," she said out loud to herself. "I never took up too much room. It was Elsie. She always needed more."

When Elsie and Mrs. Potter came back, Elsie's face was closed and unreadable. She went directly to her room and shut the door of that, too. Mrs. Potter advanced on the kitchen, discarding her purse and scarf and coat on various chairs and tables along the way. She tied an apron around her waist.

"Dinner!" she cried to herself, and opened the refrigerator door. Mary was at her elbow.

"Well, how was she? What did she say?"

"Say?" Mrs. Potter rifled in the freezer.

"Miss Fitch!" said Mary. "How is she?"

"Miss Fitch," mused Mrs. Potter, staring at a lump of frozen meat. "Miss Fitch is . . ."

She paused, and left Mary hanging, while lower down in the refrigerator, the cheese, and then the milk, and then the eggs arranged themselves in her mind.

"Omelets!" cried Mrs. Potter, inspired at last.

"Miss Fitch," she added, "is fine. She is much better. Much, much better."

"Oh, Mother," sighed Mary, for this was Mrs. Potter's standard response. It was what she always said about whatever wounded bird she had just visited. They were always much, much better.

"And we are going again tomorrow," Mrs. Potter went on. "She asked Elsie specially."

Mary said, "Oh." And then, later, softly, "Did you tell her hello from me?" But her mother was plunged into omelets by that time and would say only that Miss Fitch's head was wrapped up in bandages of some sort, which made hearing a little difficult for her.

Quite late that night, long after Mr. Potter had returned from a three-day business trip and sighed, bleary-eyed, at the omelet on his plate; long after the little ones were bounced and jostled noisily into bed; after a full moon had risen and Mrs. Potter had exclaimed and rushed outside, heedless of the cold air that poured in behind her; long, long after, Mary knocked on Elsie's door.

"Who is it?" Elsie called out, and when she heard who, "Come in," with a snap in her voice. She was sitting upright at her desk amidst a gleam of bronze. Her new pen was in her hand. The bright light from her desk lamp dazzled Mary's eyes.

"I have something," Mary began. "Sit down," ordered Elsie. Mary fidgeted and squinted to see where, and finally chose the very edge of Elsie's bed, in case she had to get up fast. The bed was tightly made, but coverless. In Mary's room, its twin lay disguised under a washable quilt printed with pink flowers. "Here is something . . ." Mary said again.

"Let's see." Elsie put out her hand. It was a card for Miss Fitch. On the front was a violin surrounded by multicolored musical notes. Inside, more notes, some flowers and, "Please get well soon, Love, Mary Potter."

"You made it," Elsie accused her.

"Yes."

"You want me to give this to her?"

"Will you?"

"Mother's going, too," said Elsie.

"I know." Mary had thought, at first, that she would give the card to her mother. But then, "It must come from Elsie," she had decided, and steeled herself for the knock on her sister's door. It must come from Elsie so that Miss Fitch would notice it, and approve of it, and not cast it instantly aside as from just another student. Elsie would make the card official, Mary thought, watching her anxiously now. Elsie was turning the card over, reading it again. Mary could see she didn't like it.

"Sure," Elsie said at last. "I'll give it to her." Then she gave the little snort that Mary dreaded. The snort was to tell Mary that not in her wildest dreams would she, Elsie Potter, ever think of giving Miss Fitch, or anyone, a silly card like this. But, if Mary wanted to, well, so much the worse for her.

Mary ignored the insult.

"Thank you," she blurted, and jumped for the door.

Elsie watched her go. She watched Mary walk all the way across the room and open the door and almost close it again. Then she spoke, softly, so softly that Mary might easily have missed it.

"What?" gasped Mary, wheeling in the doorway.

"I said, 'I know who did it,' " Elsie repeated.

"You what?"

"I know who attacked Miss Fitch," said Elsie, raising her voice a notch higher. She passed her hand over the brilliant blue cover of her notebook. "And I know why," Elsie added, turning around to face her sister.

Mary stepped back into the room and closed the door behind her.

"Why?" she asked breathlessly.

6

Why Elsie should have chosen that moment to tell about Miss Fitch, Mary could not, afterward, imagine. It was past midnight. Outside the frozen windowpanes, Grove Street slept its peaceful suburban sleep. Two miles westward, the city proper winked and blinked with lights, but they were forgotten lights, like the traffic signals that changed red, and then green, and back to red again without a soul in sight to make sense of them.

The ugly stone school buildings to which the girls would report at 8:05 the next morning were shut up. The old library nearby was dark. Further west, across the railroad tracks, crumbling warehouses well known to such as Jimmy Dee in warmer hours lay abandoned now, frozen to the core of their creaking timbers. Everything in Millport was dark, cold, bedded down, except Elsie's room with its brightly lit desk shoved into a corner. It had been a strange time to talk. But then, why should Elsie have wanted to tell at all? It made

Mary shiver to think of the journal in Elsie's desk, which all this time had been collecting secrets, who knew what secrets, or whose.

"Why are you telling me?" Mary had exclaimed. "You never tell me anything!"

"Because you should know. You especially," answered Elsie, as if she, Elsie, were some kind of white knight come gallantly out of the dark to protect her sister's virtue.

"It can't be true!" wailed Mary.

It was true, all right. "I saw it," Elsie said. She had everything written down in her journal and had only to refer to Friday, the night of December 9, or Saturday, the evening of January 7, to prove the facts.

The facts were the callers. They came to Miss Fitch's house in the evening, six times a month, seven times, sometimes three times in one week.

"But never together," said Elsie. "I'll say that for her, she's got a neat schedule."

"Callers?" Mary had asked. "What kind of callers?"

"Men, of course," said Elsie casually. But she was embarrassed and glanced away.

"Men?" Mary asked.

"Mary! Get smart for a change. You know, men! Like in lovers."

"Lovers!"

"Anyway," Elsie continued, "there are at least four or five different ones. Probably more. I couldn't always see them very well. It's dark outside when they come, and I had to stand back. I couldn't get too close to the window."

"What window?"

"Mary. Listen!"

"But, Elsie. This is crazy. Miss Fitch wouldn't . . ."

"Yes, she would," snapped Elsie. "Miss Fitch is not who you think she is. She lets people see only one side of her. She keeps the other side secret."

"But she's too old!" cried Mary. "She must be over sixty."

"Sixty exactly. And she doesn't think she's old. You know the way she dresses, so flashy and flirty."

"I like the way she dresses!" protested Mary. "I think she wears wonderful clothes."

"And she dyes her hair, too," Elsie said. "I saw the stuff in the bathroom."

"She does?"

"Oh, yes. You should see what she has upstairs. There's a whole dressing table full of lipsticks and rouge and eye makeup. She has about ten different kinds of perfume and skin cream. She's got false eyelashes, too. And false fingernails. All the stuff that women like her wear to make themselves look cheap and slinky. That's how they get their business, you know."

"What business?" asked Mary. "What do you mean, 'business'?"

Elsie sat back in her chair and gazed sadly at Mary.

"What do you think?" she said. She nudged her notebook with her elbow. "Look at the facts. I mean, one lover, okay. So what. Two lovers, well that's borderline. But four, five, six? That's a business."

Mary stared at the notebook.

"I couldn't believe it either, at first," Elsie said.

Mary opened her mouth, then shut it again without a word.

"It's actually seeing them that makes it clear," Elsie assured her. "When you're right there looking, you get the picture loud and clear. Now listen to this." She turned to the notebook, flipping pages as she found and read the entries.

" 'Friday, December 9. Man in tan Chevrolet. 6:32 P.M. New York license plates. Departs 10:48. Suit and tie. Gray hair.' "

"But did you actually see them in there. I mean, were they . . . ?"

"I saw enough," Elsie answered. "Now listen."

" 'Saturday, December 17. Brown, leatherish jacket. White shoes. 7:03 P.M. Blue Ford station wagon. Connecticut plates. Tall, skinny. Departs 11:26.'

" 'Wednesday, December 21. 7:17 P.M. Plaid pants, down vest. White Rabbit . . .' "

"White rabbit!" broke in Mary, nervously. "What's this white rabbit?"

"The car, stupid, not the person. The person was bald. And he had this kind of greasy beard. He's been there a lot of times. He's one of the regulars."

Elsie went on reading:

" 'Monday, January 2. Blue Ford station wagon is there upon arrival at 7:49 P.M. Still there at 9:30 P.M.'

" 'Saturday, January 7. Fat man, smoking, black rain coat. Arrives 8:12 P.M. Plymouth. New York plates. Still there at 10:58.'

"He was really suspicious-looking," Elsie said, glancing up. "He kept looking around over his shoulder when he walked to the house. He littered, too," she added in disgust. "He threw his cigar in the bushes. I've got it here if you want to see it."

Mary stared at the cigar. It was pretty grisly.

"Well, that's a sample," Elsie went on. "Of course, I couldn't be there every minute. Mother has a nervous fit when I get home late, so I didn't always see them leave. If they did leave, that is." She tapped her pen on a notebook page.

"They were friends, of course," Mary murmured, without conviction.

"Could be. That sure would be a lot of men callers, alone at night, just for friends," answered Elsie.

Mary turned on her angrily then.

"You're a spy," she hissed. "How could you do this? What does it prove? And anyway, I don't believe it. Miss Fitch isn't like that. She never even goes out. She goes to New York about twice a year for concerts."

"Right! And that's probably where she meets them. New York is full of creeps. It's where Mother first started loving deadbeats. There are millions of creeps down there. She picks them up. Miss Fitch is a real charmer. You've seen her in action," Elsie said bitterly. "She makes everybody love her."

"You've made this up," said Mary. "You've decided to hate her so you're making things up about her. You want me to hate her, too. That's why you're telling."

Elsie said: "Listen, Mary. I'm not making anything

up. She's a fraud, that's all. She's like one of Mother's deadbeats, only worse, because she pretends to be respectable and she's not. I know her better than you. I've seen all the signs. She's a bad person. What happened to her happens to women like her all the time."

"What happened?" cried Mary, who had completely forgotten how they had come to this discussion in the first place.

"She got beaten up by one of the men. Maybe she tried to blackmail him or something. Maybe he just got tired of her, who knows?"

"You saw that, too?" Mary asked in horror. Elsie, it seemed suddenly, was miles beyond her. Mary looked at her sister and she seemed like a wholly different animal, not related to her by a single cell.

"Well, did you?" Mary asked again. Elsie had paused. She appeared to be thinking.

"I didn't actually see it," she conceded at last. "I wasn't there that night. But I know it happened. What else could it have been? Men don't just walk in off the streets around here and beat women up for no reason. There was a reason, you can count on it."

"So, you really don't know who did it!"

"No," Elsie agreed. "But I know everything else."

Mary nodded. That was true. Elsie's notebook was full of facts. And behind the facts was Elsie, clear and practical herself, sitting at her desk under a painfully brilliant white light. Elsie wasn't the kind of person who made mistakes. Mary cupped her hands over her eyes. Her head ached.

Elsie began to tidy up her already spotless desk. She put her pen back in the pen holder and her journal back in the drawer.

"Do you still want me to give this card to Miss Fitch?"

"Well, I guess so."

There was nothing else to be said. Mary got up to go. It was late. Elsie's clock read 2 A.M.

"Why did you start spying on her anyway?" Mary asked, already resigned to whatever answer Elsie might choose to give.

"I don't know." Elsie paused. "She's French, you know."

"So what?"

"She lived in a little town outside of Paris during the war."

"What war?"

"World War Two, of course. The Nazis were there occupying France. She lived in this town. Her name isn't really Fitch. It's Fichet. She told me. Renee Fichet. She said she changed it because nobody here could pronounce Fichet. Hah!"

Was this some kind of answer? Mary rubbed her forehead.

"Look it up for yourself if you're interested. The war, I mean," said Elsie. "There are a lot of books about it in the library. You can find out things they never tell you in school."

Mary rubbed her forehead harder. Her head felt fuzzy, wrapped up in something. She thought of Miss Fitch's bandages.

"It's interesting," Elsie went on. "You can find out what life was like during the war." She watched Mary carefully, as if her words carried some special meaning. Mary gazed at her blankly.

"You can find out what some people were doing while other people were risking their lives and fighting and getting killed," Elsie said slowly, still watching.

Mary shook her head. "I don't get it," she mumbled. Elsie's eyes flicked away.

"No. You wouldn't."

Then Elsie turned back to her desk and gave Mary her profile to look at: the small nose twitched arrogantly up at the end; the chin thrust forward; the skin stretched over her cheeks, absorbing the heavy bronze color of those strange implements ranged before her.

To Mary, squinting into the light, it seemed for a moment that Elsie had turned into bronze, for she sat still and gleaming as a metal statue while the shadowy room whirled around her.

Quietly, Mary let herself out the door and tiptoed down the hall. Her own room looked cluttered, overstuffed, beside the starkness of Elsie's. She switched off her beside lamp and lay in bed. Elsie's bright light had burned into her head. When she closed her eyes, its sharp point rose up and danced inside her eyelids.

7

Elsie had not told Mary everything. Oh, no. There was more about Miss Fitch. Much more. The callers, Elsie believed, were only symptoms of another terrible disease. The callers were what Elsie had expected to see (she almost could have predicted them!) after uncovering the larger, blacker secret that Miss Fitch kept hidden beneath her charm.

This larger secret Elsie could tell no one. She could only hint: "I've been doing some research on World World Two in the library." "In the library, you can find out things they never tell you in school." Big secrets are hard to keep, no matter how much one needs to have them all to oneself. Slowly, imperceptibly, like air from a tightly bound balloon, they leak.

But Miss Fitch's secret wasn't in the library any more. Now it lay hidden, a secret within a secret, inside a drawer of Elsie's desk. Even as Mary shut the door and passed quietly down the hall to her room, Elsie's hand twitched and she longed to bring it out into the light again.

But not yet. Late as it was, Elsie must first rise from her desk to stretch, to waggle a foot that had fallen asleep, to make order of the conversation just concluded; to make order of the whole day, for that matter. She was a careful person, start to finish.

With her hands shoved deep into her jeans pockets, Elsie walked twice around the room in one direction; then, turning, twice around in the other. As she walked, all the parts of her room—the lamp and the desk, the bed and the table, the windows and the walls—revolved obligingly around her, and she thought how perfectly arranged they all were. Everything was put just where it should be. (But, there was a wrinkle in the bed where Mary had sat. She smoothed it down in passing.) Nothing was there by mistake, but only because she wanted it there.

Elsie was glad she had told, that was clear to her immediately. She felt lighter all over. Not that she needed to tell. Certainly not. But to see Mary mooning over Miss Fitch like a lovesick dog, to watch her day after day being deceived, to be honest, it had made Elsie nervous. It was as if Elsie, by not telling about the callers, was telling a lie.

"So there, you old witch," Elsie said out loud, rounding the carpet a fourth and final time. She was speaking to Miss Fitch: to Miss Fitch wired up in her hospital bed across town; to Miss Fitch, wearing a horrid white turban that gave her skin a yellowish shine; to Miss Fitch, without makeup, leaning queerly against the propped-up pillows, as if she were pinned to them.

"Thank you for coming," Miss Fitch had said hoarsely that afternoon, trying to give Elsie a special look of welcome. Elsie had refused it by turning her face to the windows. She wanted to look, but not while Miss Fitch was watching. She wanted to see exactly what had happened to Miss Fitch, to measure its shockingness. Elsie was curious to know the details of being beaten up, and later while her mother gushed and chirped, she had stolen small glances at the plaster-cast arm hauled awkwardly up in traction, and at the limp legs under the blanket, and at an evil-looking scrape that ran up the inside of Miss Fitch's unbroken arm.

The scrape, being bare, appeared more dreadful than the other covered wounds. It spoke of violence and, by extension, of fear. It made Miss Fitch a victim of attack and not someone who was recovering from surgery or disease. Elsie felt a twinge of sympathy when she looked at the scrape. But she had only to raise her eyes to meet Miss Fitch's questioning ones to freeze herself again.

Boldly, steadily, Miss Fitch regarded her, asking without words, over and over:

"Why? What is wrong? Talk to me!" They knew each other well enough to talk through silence. It had been one of the pleasures of their alliance. But Elsie would not talk. In the hospital, she turned her eyes away, turned her back, looked out the window.

Now, in her late-night room, Elsie stood before her desk and her hand moved, was pulled, toward a certain drawer, toward a certain corner far back in the drawer, toward the secret she had not told Mary, the black, secret center of Miss Fitch.

It was a photograph. Elsie drew it out at last. She flattened it carefully on her desk, for it was shabby, creased in places, from having been handled too often. She moved it close to the light and examined it for details, as if it were a portrait whose subtle composition might hold secret meaning.

There was a face in the photograph, but it had never yet allowed Elsie to enter. Turn it this way, turn it that, it rebuffed scrutiny. The face never changed, although at times Elsie had thought it must change, must be changed by all her looking and knowing. It was the same as the day in the library last November when Elsie had first come across the picture in the book containing photographs of World War II.

World War II. Elsie had heard about it, of course, even before Miss Fitch. She knew it was bad. The Civil War was bad, too. (In history class, Elsie had listened to a tape dramatizing the Battle of Gettysburg: "General Meade, sir! The Confederates have broken through. They make for the ridge!" Explosions, followed by screams and groans.)

All wars were bad, but until Miss Fitch they were anonymous too, and old-fashioned like history itself. They were a matter of dates and treaties that Elsie memorized for school tests.

Miss Fitch's war had no dates and no treaties. It broke slowly into Elsie's mind as a series of stray comments that Miss Fitch tossed off during violin lessons.

"We could not get sheet music during the war."

Or, when Elsie arrived one day eating an orange:

"Oranges! Such plenty, now. But, then? Oh, then! I did not see an orange for four years. And at night? I dreamed for oranges."

Another time, Miss Fitch began:

"A friend I had who died during the war . . ."

"How? Killed, you mean? Shot?" Elsie asked.

Miss Fitch had brushed her off quickly.

"No, no. Just died. She was an old woman, like I am old now."

"You're not old, Miss Fitch!" Elsie had cried. They had been friends then. They had begun to understand each other. Miss Fitch understood that Elsie could not be teased or hounded, like other students, into a better performance. She had her dignity.

Elsie learned not to ask Miss Fitch about her war. It was a subject Miss Fitch did not care to discuss, she saw. Respectfully, she let Miss Fitch's comments pass by her.

Respectfully, but—in the library that fall, Elsie began a small investigation. She checked out a book about World War II, read it through in her room and returned it. She took out another. She began to see how Miss Fitch's war fitted in, how Miss Fitch herself had been part of World War II. It was exciting. *France During the Occupation. The French Resistance, 1941–45.* She read with increasing interest, whole Saturday afternoons in the library. And after school, hidden between the tall book shelves, she sat cross-legged on the library floor, too fascinated even to carry the books to a table. Too fascinated, and also—too appalled.

The war was horrible. There were heroes in it, and stories of great daring. School children carried messages. Women ran secret radio stations. Men dropped by parachute behind enemy lines. But beneath the daring was horror: murder and torture and unspeakable fear. Chaos, too. Who was a friend? Who was an enemy? People told on their neighbors. Traitors collaborated with the Nazis. Whole families were marched away, betrayed by spies and double agents. There were times when Elsie, crouched in the library stacks, looked up at the long, even rows of shelves around her and let her eyes cling to them for relief. She would listen to the squeak of a chair, to the calm murmur of voices, and feel grateful for the immense peace and order in that library.

And later, arriving exactly on time for her weekly lesson with Miss Fitch ("Order. Order!"), Elsie watched her teacher with new interest. That fall, she practiced hard on her violin. She was getting better, and knew it.

"Amazing!" Miss Fitch had cried. "You are amazing!"

This pleased Elsie as much as anything ever had pleased her.

Then, one day in early November, Elsie found the photograph. The picture book was a large volume, rather thin for its size, but heavy. It was marked "R" for "Reference," and could not be taken out of the library. Elsie had looked through the book several times before, and came back to it that day with a little thrill of dread. The book showed scenes from the war, and, because the pages were large, the black and white pictures were big and bold and full of detail. Elsie examined them carefully.

There were bodies sprawled at the sides of roads, their legs flung at sickening angles. There were terrified children peering through walls blown apart by bombs. There were buildings actually crumbling, blowing up before your eyes, while people ran screaming in all directions. And there were country scenes in which every leaf on every tree was gone, blasted off, Elsie supposed, so that the trees stood about naked and frightened, pointing skinny arms to the sky.

Elsie was turning these pages slowly when she came upon the photograph. Even then, she had nearly gone on because there seemed nothing very violent or awful about it at first. The picture showed the street of an ordinary French town teeming with townsfolk. They were everyday sort of people: mothers holding the hands of children, and men wearing plain work clothes; grandmothers in long skirts with scarves tied around their broad faces; older children running ahead by themselves, scampering ahead as children do to keep up with a parade.

Well, it was a parade, in a way, Elsie saw. Celebration was in the air. The German armies which had occupied France for four years had been defeated.

"Liberation!" Elsie read the headline below the photograph. "And Old Scores Are Settled."

She had not understood. She had stopped to look more closely at the picture.

Two rough wooden carts—old-fashioned farm carts— were being pulled down the street by two solid farm horses. In the carts—strange—stood women. Two women in one; one woman in the second. They held babies in their arms and, what was stranger still, their hair was all shaved off. To Elsie, they looked hardly like women at all. They looked more like men, like the skinny-headed men in other photos who were prisoners of war, and whose heads had been shaved to disgrace them.

Elsie had leaned forward on her elbows, then. Below the headline was a caption:

"Surrounded by jeering crowds in a town near Paris, accused French collaborators are driven through the streets bearing the burdens of their shame: their German-sired infants. Minutes before, their heads had been shorn by their angry countrymen. Other female fraternizers had swastikas painted on their foreheads."

Only then did Elsie examine the faces of the women. She wanted to see what sorts of women would do such a thing, and why. She wanted to see beneath their faces into their minds, where hidden thoughts bubbled and churned. Were they ashamed? shocked? angry? Elsie looked at the faces of the women and saw . . . Miss Fitch! Recognition came like a thunderclap. Her face was younger, her scalp almost bald, but this served only to make the familiar features stand out more clearly.

Elsie saw the thick, black hyphens of the eyebrows. ("So very French," someone had told her once, commenting on Miss Fitch's appearance. They had looked merely odd, rather exotic, to Elsie.) She saw the cheekbones plunging back toward the ears. She saw the long, proud neck. She knew it was Miss Fitch although no names were given.

In the corner of the first cart she stood, leaning against the wooden side, swaying a bit. There was a swaying look on her face, too, a dizzy, half-blank expression. As if someone had struck her, Elsie thought, and she was just beginning to recover.

And she had been struck! Elsie saw the spatter and drool of some soft vegetable on her skirt. Then Elsie had understood why she was leaning forward in that odd manner. Miss Fitch was shielding the bundle clutched in her arms against other flying missiles. Her baby!

Elsie's first instinct was to hide the photograph, to protect it from surrounding eyes. (Or was she really protecting her own eyes?) In the library that day she was stacking books around her, covering the frightening page with school notes before she knew what she was doing. Only later, huddled behind that barricade, did she decide to remove the photograph from the library altogether. The picture did not belong in the library, she decided. Right or wrong, mistake or not, it must be taken away, out of public view for private study.

But to steal a book? This was no small venture. To

steal was a crime and Elsie was not a criminal. To tear the picture out then, to mutilate? Elsie's stomach churned. She sat up in her chair and surveyed the library. The chairs at the reading tables were mostly vacant. Three tables ahead, an old man in a ragged jacket licked his finger and turned the page of a magazine. Off to her left, two girls whispered together over a notebook. A librarian sighed behind the check-out counter across the room, and wiped her eyes with the back of her hand.

Warily, Elsie opened the photograph book. The terrible picture nestled inside, black and white, clear as real life. Elsie made her decision and began at once.

Using the edge of her thumbnail, she drew a line down the side of the picture where it attached to the binding, then across the picture's bottom edge. The nail was too dull to cut, but it made a long furrow on the paper. Over and over Elsie worked the furrow with her nail. When its depth suited her, she glanced up again to inspect the room. Her heart thumped.

Elsie bent her head and began to tear the photograph from the book. The noise was deafening. The old man's head shot up. He gazed about him. She tore frantically. The photograph's bottom edge did not part evenly. The tear left the furrow and wandered down into the print below, and up, with jagged leaps, into the picture. The page was ruined. With a last shriek of paper, Elsie freed the photograph. Then she sat perfectly still and waited to see what would happen.

Nothing happened. No one was looking. The man's face had dropped into his magazine again. Elsie's hands shook. She closed the ruined picture book and placed it on the table. She tucked the photograph inside a school binder. She gathered her other books and her book bag and, rising unsteadily to her feet, she walked out of the library.

If Elsie had had a friend, she would have shown the photograph to her. Then, perhaps, they could have whispered over it, and made up stories about it, and laughed the shock away: "What a mystery! Is that really Miss Fitch?"

But Elsie didn't have that kind of friend. She meant to have one, even several. She tried sometimes. In the end, people her age always did something or said something that made Elsie shrink away from them. They were childish and disorganized—always forgetting their books in class, or losing their assignments. For their benefit, teachers repeated instructions ten times over and devised study hall rules that insulted Elsie's accute sense of responsibility. The school was run like a kindergarten: don't talk; don't run; five minutes to go to the bathroom—all for their infantile benefit. And they were unreliable, muddle-headed. They thought one thing one moment and another the next. They talked behind each other's backs. They laughed at other people's mistakes and took no notice of their own.

The girls Elsie knew screamed about nothing and hid around corners where they could watch the boys talking in groups. The boys shoved knowingly against each other and sneered back. To Elsie, this seemed disgusting in some way, cheap and unnatural, like the love songs that moaned from the transistor radios slung from their shoulders during recess.

"Hey, baby!" called the boys. "Come on over here. We got something you wanta see." Disgusting love-song talk. Elsie was embarrassed to hear it, embarrassed to see other girls saunter over, smiling queer, self-conscious smiles: "So, David. What'd you end up doing last night?" Couldn't they see how they degraded themselves?

"Ah! They are so young!" Miss Fitch had exclaimed when Elsie had brought the matter up one day, long before her research in the library, before the callers. "Full of youth and high spirits and not knowing yet what the world is all about. So unsure of themselves! They must make it up with loud talk."

Elsie understood, but she would not be part of it.

"No. Not you," Miss Fitch agreed. And turning to look at Elsie fondly: "You. You are as I was. Oh, what a child that was! So stern and proud and wanting all the time to be perfect. Wanting the world perfect too, I think. I'll tell you, I wished only to get away from the others. I wished to get out."

"Yes!" Elsie had cried. "That is just what I feel!"

"Yes," said Miss Fitch, and they had smiled at each other.

This was the Miss Fitch, the young Renee Fichet, whom Elsie now tried to reconcile with the woman in the terrible photograph. And while the two images warred in her mind, she could not go to Miss Fitch either. She could not breathe a word to her. She could only watch her closely, gathering more evidence.

The photograph grew large in Elsie's mind. It obsessed her. Almost every night during the long winter she drew it out of her desk drawer to look again.

"Accused collaborator." Elsie knew what that was. "Burden of shame." Elsie stared at the baby, shocked. The charge against Miss Fitch was awesome. For Miss Fitch had been like Elsie. She had said so. She believed like Elsie in perfection, in trying for the best and rejecting the second rate. She had believed, and believed now, in independence. Didn't she live alone, supporting herself and keeping her own counsel? Elsie admired that. Quite apart from the violin lessons, the constant quest under Miss Fitch's sharp eyes for better and then best, besides the lessons, Elsie loved being inside her house, her rooms. It was not a large house, nor was it fashionably decorated. But the house was Miss Fitch's own, a private place she had won from the world and could arrange and live in just as she pleased.

"Can I come sometimes? You know, just to visit?" Elsie had asked Miss Fitch shyly during the first year of her lessons.

"But, of course!" Miss Fitch was almost too pleased, too eager. And Elsie *had* gone. She had studied in the strange dining room with its swooping white curtains while Miss Fitch conducted lessons in her living room. And later, they had made coffee together, a rich aromatic brew that Miss Fitch stewed in an odd-shaped metal pot, then poured, steaming, into two small elegant mugs nestled on two tiny saucers. The mugs were white and fluted up the sides like Greek columns Elsie had seen in pictures of ancient ruins. The coffee tasted bitter, mysterious.

"It is a very special mixture. I grind the beans myself," Miss Fitch had told her the first time, never even asking if Elsie drank coffee, if she was allowed to drink it. At home, Elsie's parents spooned instant coffee into cups of hot water.

"Where does it come from?" Elsie had asked. It was what she wanted to ask about everything in Miss Fitch's house: about the strange cuts of cheese she kept under a glass cover on the kitchen counter; about the panels of lace hung down the double doors leading to the living room; about the fringed lamp shades, the densely patterned wallpaper, the unfamiliar plants on the windowsills.

Wherever Elsie put her eyes there was a difference. It came out of Miss Fitch and shot through all the rooms of her house, making them peculiar, a special mixture all her own.

"But were you never married?" Elsie had asked. "Not even long ago?"

"No. Never. Not even once. Does this seem odd?"

"Oh, no! Not at all!"

"Marriage was not for me," said Miss Fitch. "Not in the cards, as they say. I had my career, you see. I moved about. I made friends, many good friends. At times, I thought, 'Yes. Perhaps marriage.' But then, well. It is hard to remember exactly why, but I chose not to have it."

Elsie had nodded. She liked the way Miss Fitch confided in her, as if they were equals, ageless.

"I like to be on my own, too," she had said. "I don't have plans to get married ever. But I have plans," she'd added hastily.

They talked over the coffee. Oh, talked! Of people and places. Miss Fitch was extremely well-traveled. She had toured as a concert violinist with an orchestra: Europe, Russia, South America. She understood things. She knew things that people in Millport would never know. She made the world open up, and sparkle.

"A concert violinist!" sighed Elsie.

"I've had some adventures," said Miss Fitch, with a twinkle in her eye. What adventures? Elsie was dying to hear them. Miss Fitch kept corridors of mystery around her, though. She spoke sparingly of the personal events in her life. "Ah, but life itself is an adventure," she would say, and Elsie had understood. If she hadn't completely understood before her research in the library, she understood afterward.

"How did you happen to come here?" Elsie asked, in wonder. Miss Fitch had smiled and answered in her own way.

"Who would not want to live in this beautiful country?" she said. "Everything is here: fine houses, fine people, fine music. And peace, oceans of peace. To live in a strong country, it is what every person wants. I had traveled enough. I wanted to settle down. I chose America. I knew I would be happy here, and safe."

Safe. Before the photograph, Elsie had known exactly what Miss Fitch meant. She had approved of her patriotic answer. Afterward . . . She stared at the photograph and understood nothing. Up high in her mind dwelt Miss Fitch, a strong-shining star. Down low, crept the picture. She could not put them together. She kept them apart. She watched each carefully to see what would happen next. Then, something happened.

Elsie was late. It was an evening in late November. She had said she would help Miss Fitch in the afternoon, after school. She had promised—what was it?— to help her move a bookcase. Something. Miss Fitch needed help from time to time.

"Living alone," she had explained once, "without relatives nearby, I must depend on my friends to help."

Elsie was proud to be chosen. And she was never late. She was not like her mother who was always late. But, this time, she was kept late at school. Play rehearsal. It went on and on, not her fault, making her late. Two hours late.

She ran up the walk to Miss Fitch's house on the way home to apologize: "So sorry! It wasn't my fault!"

The living room was strangely, dimly lit. She glanced

in the front window. Miss Fitch never shut the blinds. It was part of her feeling safe, perhaps. Elsie glanced in the window to see if Miss Fitch was home, and there they were, framed, still, two shadowy black-and-white forms half-turned toward each other on the couch.

His hair was white and wavy, slippery-looking. Elsie hated him on sight—the enemy. His arm was around Miss Fitch's shoulders. Her face was lifted to his. They clung together, and kissed, two pale ghost-bodies in the webby half light.

It wasn't love but information their lips passed back and forth. Elsie saw it, just as clearly as if this were another photograph in the big library book. She understood how it had been, back then and now. There was no difference. They traded secrets while around them innocent people went about their business of eating dinner, talking, washing dishes, betrayed. They were conspirators. No. Collaborators. This was collaborating! Elsie stumbled back, away from the window.

From that moment, she was a spy. She spied on Wednesday afternoon after basketball and on Friday nights coming home late from play practice. On Saturday evenings while the other Potters watched television or played Monopoly, Elsie walked, regardless of the cold, and nearly always ended up outside Miss Fitch's house. She gave up going to Miss Fitch's dining room to study. She gave up violin lessons. She spied instead, through December, January, into February.

Jimmy Dee saw her. She became another of the daily obstacles that he learned with craft and stealth to circumvent. In the waning light of early evening, in the dead dark of night, he remembered to look for Elsie's small shape near the front of the house, and to avoid it in the same manner as he would have avoided a street lamp or a car idling at the curb. To Jimmy Dee, Elsie's lurking form was neither man nor woman nor child nor ghost. It was danger only. Or rather, it was a shape that radiated a more intense danger than usual. He passed by and forgot it. Elsie never saw him. Her post was a tree near the middle of the lawn. She dared go no nearer.

There were nights, many nights, when, unaware, they watched the house together. But while Miss Fitch's solitary playing warmed Jimmy Dee, Elsie's heart slowly froze against it. Jimmy Dee waited for the music and slunk away at the first sight of a visitor. Elsie waited for the men. Beside them, the music sounded preposterous to her, and later, demented.

Slowly, everything that had been beautiful about Miss Fitch turned ugly. And the violin became an ugly instrument, and the act of playing became an ugly act.

"The old witch. The fraud," Elsie hissed to herself, over and over, outside the house. But beneath these words were others which she did not say out loud, which she only thought: liar, coward, collaborator. Frightening words. And the most frightening of all: traitor.

9

Amidst shrieking sirens, in the glare of frantic lights, Miss Fitch had gone to the hospital. Now she returned without drama, sitting pale but upright in the hushed interior of a slow-driven ambulance. A pot of pink geraniums greeted her on the doorstep. "Welcome Home! From the Potters," the tag read.

Miss Fitch paused to pluck a bit of tissue from her bag. She blew her nose and went on into the house to make a thank-you phone call, to issue—"Yes. Come tomorrow. I am fine. Fine!"—an unconvincingly hearty invitation.

How was she really? Nobody knew.

"Tired, I should think," said Mrs. Potter, drawing on her vast experience of recuperations. "Hospitals are nervous places. The body is well tended but the head is left to fend for itself."

"It's about time she came home," declared Elsie. "She's been there for eleven solid days."

"Heavens! Has it been that long?" asked Mrs. Potter.

"Well, she went in on Wednesday, February 28, and today, if you notice, is Sunday, March 11. That's eleven days," Elsie said.

Mrs. Potter smiled and ruffled her daughter's hair.

"That's my Elsie," she said, proudly. "Always exact down to the minute. How did I, from my muddle, produce such a child?"

Mary, standing nearby, frowned at both of them.

"You sure have been counting days for someone who doesn't care," she said to Elsie.

"Anybody can read a calendar," sniffed Elsie. She wasn't going with Mary and Mrs. Potter to visit Miss Fitch the next afternoon. Two visits were enough for her. Enough for Miss Fitch too, it seemed. She hadn't asked for Elsie again.

"Let Mother go if she wants," Elsie told Mary privately, later that night. "It's Mother's job to go. That's what she does with her life, visits deadbeats. What would Mother do all day if she wasn't poking into places where she isn't wanted."

"But she *is* wanted!" cried Mary. "How can you say such a thing about Mother?"

"Well, then," said Elsie cruelly, "you're not wanted. So why are you going?"

That hurt. Mary blushed.

"I'm going because . . . because . . . I want to," she stammered. Elsie snorted.

"And because," Mary glared at her sister, "because I don't believe one thing you've said about Miss Fitch. Not one thing!"

"You mean you do believe it and you're going to look for yourself," Elsie replied, smiling.

Mary fled, then. She ran upstairs to hide her face in her room. And to clench her fist and pound it into a pillow. For Elsie's words had truth in them. Not that Mary believed Elsie's facts. No, she didn't. She couldn't. But:

"Mother? Elsie has been watching Miss Fitch and . . ." Mary had almost said it a hundred times during the past few days.

"Mother? Do you think Miss Fitch would . . . ?" Mary wanted to tell. She needed someone to think it out for her. She wanted to hear her mother say, "Ridiculous! Whatever has gotten into Elsie?"

Mary had not told. She had gone upstairs to work on her homework instead, or she had washed her hair. ("Why is there never any hot water in this house?" bellowed Mr. Potter.)

She had cleaned out her room, old clothes, old stuffed animals, an ugly leftover toy chest she'd been using as a hamper.

"Want this?" she asked Roo.

"Okay."

They hauled the toy chest into Roo's side of the room she shared with Heidi.

Heidi said: "Oh, no! Not that thing. I'm telling Mother. I can't even breathe in here with all Roo's stuff."

But it stayed. Roo worked it out. Mary's room looked bigger suddenly. And emptier.

"What should I wear to Miss Fitch's house?" Mary asked her mother. Strange, but as the hour of the visit drew nearer, that was the question which worried her most.

"I don't have anything!" cried Mary.

"But, here. What's this? I see a whole closet full of things," coaxed Mrs. Potter.

"Everything is too old or too small," wailed Mary. "And nothing goes together."

She was thinking of Miss Fitch's clothes, wondering suddenly about them. Weren't they wonderful? Of course they were. Everybody remarked on it. She wore the most amazing dresses: soft, flowing, exotically draped things that announced themselves boldly and were meant to be noticed. (But not the way Elsie said.) Parisian, Mary guessed they were, or Italian; cut from fabrics unknown to the American department stores, in styles born of some wild, foreign imagination. Not that Miss Fitch's clothes were the latest fashion. They weren't even new. They were like Miss Fitch herself, charming and a little strange, from sources unexplainable and faintly mysterious.

"I am fat," Mary told her mother. "Fat, pure and simple. And getting fatter."

"Not a bit," protested Mrs. Potter, and her own ample form gave the look of truth to it. "Here's a blouse I've always liked," she said, holding it up.

"That thing."

"And your blue skirt. There!"

"Horrible," said Mary. But she put it on.

"But what shoes?" asked Mary. She could decide nothing. Her mind was in a froth of uncertainty. "Oh, Mother! How can I possibly go in my old . . ."

"These shoes," Mrs. Potter told her gently, drawing out some party pumps from far back in the closet.

"Well, all right. Not too dressy?"

"Just perfect. And now hurry! I said we'd be there at four o'clock."

Mary combed her hair straight down at the sides, examined herself a final time in the mirror and dashed for her coat.

Elsie was nowhere to be seen. But Mary had the feeling as she got into the car with her mother that from some dim window in the house, tucked behind some curtain, Elsie was watching.

10

Miss Fitch was at the door to greet them before they were halfway up the steps of her porch.

"Here you are! Welcome!" She flung the door wide for them to pass.

"I've put some tea in the living room. Tea is what you like, isn't it? Grace, my love! You've brought your famous brownies. What a dear." She swept her good arm around Mrs. Potter and brought their cheeks together in the hall. Mary stood aside, surprised. She had not thought they knew each other so well.

"And Mary. Come in. Sit down. I have waited all day for this and now, here you are." About Elsie, she said nothing. "I am so very happy to see you both!"

She did not look happy. She looked terrible. Her face was so old and thin that Mary hardly dared to glance at her. She wore a plain, wilted, beige wrapper over some sort of bulky sweater. At first, Mary thought she had shrunk. But it was only that she hadn't put her high-heeled shoes on. And her hair!

"There, now. Sit down. Tell me all the news. What a place that hospital. So full of nurses and . . . and . . . of antiseptics." She chose the word doubtfully, as if she were learning the language again. Her smile wasn't right.

"No. Don't say a word, not a word about this ugly face. I have not dressed. I am a little—what do you say?—under the weather. I am a little under the weather, still."

She sank into a chair and gazed bleakly at Mary. "And they have taken my hair. In order to treat the wound. You see!" She gestured toward her head, an apology of sorts.

Mary did see. The hair was cropped close and, in one place, half hidden by a scarf she'd bound over her head, seemed to be shaved off completely.

"It is nothing. Nothing!" said Miss Fitch, too loudly. "But bad to look at, I think. The cut is very much better."

"I am glad the bandages have come off," put in Mrs. Potter. "That didn't take long, did it?"

Miss Fitch smiled at her, a scarecrow grin.

"Darling, Gracie." She turned to Mary. "She has been my best customer at the hospital. All those hours lying there, and then this bright face through the door. I haven't said thank you very well. I know it!"

"Of course you have!" cried Mrs. Potter.

But, no. No. Miss Fitch was pressing Mrs. Potter's hand, smiling out such intense gratitude that her face cracked and buckled like an old piece of rubber.

Mary looked away, embarrassed. She felt she was intruding on private ground, spying even, like Elsie. Miss Fitch was not meant to be seen this way, without makeup, without her beautiful clothes, and so undignified, thanking Mrs. Potter like a desperate child. Her movements were awkward, too, out of kilter because of the heavy cast on her right arm. It hung across her chest at an odd angle. She hitched herself toward the teapot and attempted to pour tea into a cup.

"I'll do that!" sang out Mrs. Potter. "You rest yourself."

"My second best customer," Miss Fitch went on, after the tea had been passed around, "was the police."

"The police!" Mrs. Potter leaned forward on the couch, all concern. "You haven't said a word about that!"

"I was not supposed to say a word," replied Miss Fitch. She dipped her head to sip unsteadily from the cup in her left hand. "But now, home at last . . ." She looked up, blank-eyed.

"Have they," Mary began, "have they found, you know . . ."

"Oh, no," said Miss Fitch. "The investigation goes on. And me, well, I am not very helpful." She gazed across at them queerly, her head bent to one side.

"Well, of course not!" said Mrs. Potter. "The shock of it all. The utter chaos. How can they expect you to remember all at once. I wouldn't remember myself."

"Exactly," said Miss Fitch, with a crack in her voice

that brought Mary's eyes straight to her face. "A terrible shock," Miss Fitch repeated, as if she had just now thought of it. "And one does not want to remember, so, of course, one doesn't."

"But, you must remember something!" blurted Mary, then put her hand over her mouth to stop herself.

Miss Fitch's eyes slid over her and fell to the floor. "Yes. Something. I remember . . . some things."

"Hush, Mary," said her mother, and they sat in silence for a long moment.

"We were speaking of the police," said Miss Fitch, at last. "Yes. Those police. They press. They pick for detail. They look for witnesses. My neighbors have been interviewed." She frowned with her mouth, pushing the lower lip up so that the sides curved down. And suddenly Mary saw what the trouble was. It wasn't the lack of makeup. It was Miss Fitch's eyes. For though she smiled and frowned, her eyes never changed. They peered out between their lids with a sort of dull, secretive gaze.

"I have never liked the police," muttered Miss Fitch, half to herself, and for a moment, Mary saw her face take on the same horrid dullness as her eyes. It was a covered-up look, watchful. It frightened Mary.

"Yes, yes!" Mrs. Potter was saying. "I would be worried myself by an investigation."

Miss Fitch moved, crablike, toward her cup.

"Of course, the police are necessary," said Mrs. Potter. "We all understand that they must do their jobs. And, of course, they must find the person who did this terrible thing. He must be brought in before he does more harm. He was a big man, did you say? You surprised him, most likely, and he lashed out. Are you sure, now you are home again, that nothing was taken?"

Miss Fitch merely shrugged. Mary stared at her, struck suddenly by her odd way of answering. Well, wasn't it odd? Most people, Mary thought, would want their attackers caught quickly. They would want justice done, be more frightened, even, if the case were not resolved, lest the criminal come back again.

Miss Fitch appeared indifferent to this. She looked worn-out suddenly. Her face seemed to grow thinner, paler, as she listened to Mrs. Potter's bubbling explanations.

"He must be caught," Mrs. Potter was saying. "But, naturally, police investigations are upsetting. Not conducive to clear thought. It will all come to you now that you are home, among your own things."

Was that it? Was it that she couldn't remember? Or did she remember everything, all too well. Was she protecting someone? Mary watched the older woman's face.

Miss Fitch was different, Mary decided. It was not just that she looked different, but inside something had changed. Or had the difference always been there? "The old fraud," Elsie had said. Was she?

Then, just as Mary's doubt rose up and reached out wildly for an answer (Elsie's answer!)—just as she felt herself swing away from this queer, secretive Miss Fitch and set foot on an opposite shore—just then,

Miss Fitch sat up abruptly and smiled her own smile. It was warm, confiding and utterly open.

"Ah, well. What can you do?" Miss Fitch shrugged again, but this time it was a philosophical, good-natured gesture.

"One does one's best." She reached across the table and took Mary's clammy hand in hers.

"Life!" she announced, smiling wryly. "One moment you think you have it all rolled up safely in the palm of your hand." She rolled Mary's hand inside her own.

"One minute you understand and can make order from it, and the next—poof! Something like this happens and all is head over heels. Then you must start again to make sense of yourself. Oh, yes. I've been through it before. You must try not to be afraid, try not to be bitter. You go forward as best you can. Well! It is wonderful in a way, isn't it? You learn and learn."

Miss Fitch glanced over at Mrs. Potter and gave her an impish wink.

"I have learned, for instance, never to open my door to a rampaging attacker in the night!"

There was a pause. Then they all burst out laughing. Miss Fitch rocked back and forth giggling, and Mrs. Potter nearly spilled her tea, and Mary laughed—she couldn't help it—until the tears came to her eyes. And as she laughed, the strange woman across the table from her blurred and wobbled through the tears, and finally came into focus again as Miss Fitch. The same, wonderful Miss Fitch. Clothes or no clothes.

Makeup or none. There was not a bit of difference after all. Elsie was wrong, so very wrong! Mary laughed harder when she thought how wrong her sister was, and she was still laughing a little as she drove home from Miss Fitch's house with her mother.

"What an extraordinary woman!" Mrs. Potter exclaimed. "What a wise and thoroughly marvelous person she is. She makes me glad to be living along with her. Perhaps it's that she's French and can see from different sides, through two languages, when we have only one to interpret the world."

"Maybe," said Mary.

"Or was it the war?" mused Mrs. Potter.

"The war?"

"I was looking at her and thinking over tea. She distrusts the police. She is afraid of investigations. It made me remember where she came from. I don't know anything about it, really. One hears things, you know, and in connection with her I have heard that she was right there, living near Paris, during the worst of the war. I was thinking. To have gone through that and come away whole, well, it would make a person extraordinary just to have done it."

"But that was so long ago," said Mary. "Everybody has forgotten about it now."

"Maybe not," her mother said. "Miss Fitch was a young woman during the war, a teen-ager not much older than you. I imagine she remembers many things."

"Has she told you anything?"

"No. People talk. I've heard that the war was hard

on her. Someone said she had a brother who died in a concentration camp."

"Miss Fitch had a brother?"

"Or he was killed fighting. I'm not sure."

Mary looked sharply at her mother.

"Killed fighting?" she repeated. The phrase rang a bell in her head.

"Elsie is studying the war," Mary said, after a minute.

"Is she?" Mrs. Potter was drifting off to her own thoughts.

"At the library," Mary added. "There are books about it in the library. Elsie said you could find out what some people were doing while other people were . . ." Mary stopped.

"Find out what?" asked Mrs. Potter, absently.

But Mary didn't answer. Outside the car window, the houses of Grove Street flickered past her eyes like an old-time movie.

11

Mary did not like libraries. Their silence and whispers unsettled her. The rooms were too big, too full of corners, like a maze. Mary could never tell who might be watching her from behind some shelf. Or maybe it was the books themselves that watched, heavy with knowledge and knowing. In the library, Mary spent as much time glancing over her shoulder, peering down shadowy aisles, as she did reading. She couldn't study there the way Elsie did. But she knew how to use the catalogs, how to get around. The World War II books were in the 940s section. There were hundreds.

Mary gazed uncertainly at the shelves and wondered where to begin. A week had passed since Miss Fitch's tea party, a week in which Mary had labored over an English essay on "*The Scarlet Letter*, by Nathaniel Hawthorne—Morality Tale or Psychological Romance?" It was a dreadful assignment from beginning to end. ("First, we must define our terms, mustn't we?" her English teacher had informed the class smugly.)

"I don't believe that stories like this should be made to have terms," Mary had told her mother one night, after two hours of struggling with the writing. "Everything in them is so slippery, you can't figure out what the author meant. Do you think that Hawthorne really knew himself?"

"I must have read that book," Mrs. Potter replied. "But I can't remember a thing about it."

Now, for better or worse, Mary's composition was turned in and she had time to think again. That afternoon, she was in the library to look into Miss Fitch's war, or was it Elsie's war?, and she found that she was more curious about it than ever. What had Elsie been reading to start her spying on Miss Fitch and making up stories about her?

Mary examined a brimming book rack. She glanced nervously up and down the aisle. Finally, she chose the largest volume she could see, with some idea that larger might be better for a first stab at information. The book seemed to be composed mostly of photographs. A piece of lined notepaper stuck out from between the pages, a welcoming sight, somehow.

Mary carried the book to a library table, sat down and began to turn the pages. Around her, the library sighed and echoed sighs, creaked and echoed. Somewhere out of sight, a pen clattered on the floor, a drawer shut. Mary put her elbows on the table and bent low over the photograph book, reading captions.

"German armored divisions enter Belgium," she read. "British naval vessels off Dunkirk begin troup evacuation." "In Paris, a French family prepares for flight as news of the invasion spreads."

Invasion! Which invasion was that, exactly? And how would it feel, Mary wondered, to be invaded? And what was this piece of notepaper poked out inconveniently from between the pages so that one's hand kept running into it? And why not pull it out, clear it out of the way? Except the handwriting on it looked familiar to her suddenly, and what place in the book was it marking? Or was it marking anything? She peeked quickly to see.

Mary pounded on Elsie's door.

"Elsie?" she called. "Elsie!" Inside the room, a chair leg squeaked. Light footsteps came across the rug. Elsie opened the door and looked out warily. She had been writing. The fierce bronze pen was in her hand.

"Elsie?"

"Well, what!"

"You have something. I want to see it."

"What do you mean?"

"I think it's a picture," said Mary. She was out of breath and panting. Her hair had the washed-back look of a long-distance runner. She leaned against the door frame and gasped for air.

"Sorry," panted Mary. She mopped her upper lip with her hand. "I've been running."

Elsie watched her coolly. "You sure are in great shape."

"It was mostly uphill."

Mary had been carrying her school books, too. Now she bent and let them fall in a jumble outside the door.

"I've been to the library," she told Elsie.

"Come in, please," Elsie said, strange formality in her voice.

Mary walked past. She sat on the bed.

"Miss Fitch is in it, isn't she?"

"In what?"

"You know."

Elsie crossed the room slowly. She sat down at her desk.

"Yes," she answered. "She's in it."

"Can I see?"

"Okay." Elsie didn't seem angry. She opened her desk drawer.

"Wait a minute." Mary got up again and went to look through the books outside the door. She held up a piece of paper.

"Your writing," she said. "I found it in the photo book. It's from science, I think."

"Thanks." Elsie checked it over. "Was there anything else?"

"Nope."

Elsie felt around inside her drawer.

"You didn't tear out the caption," Mary said. "That's how I—"

"Here it is," Elsie said, suddenly. She didn't hand the photograph over, though. She sat at her desk and stared at it until Mary came and looked over her shoulder.

"She's here," said Elsie, pointing. They examined the figure in the wooden cart together silently.

"It's her, all right," Mary said at last.

"How did you know I took it?" asked Elsie. She sounded relieved, respectful, as if Mary finally had done something she approved of.

"I found your science notes right there, sticking out. It's strange. I was looking for Miss Fitch, or trying, anyway, to imagine her in the war. She had a brother—did you know?—who was killed in the war. I was trying to imagine how that was. All those pictures. It was pretty bad, wasn't it? She must have been scared the whole time. They arrested you if you did anything suspicious. They shot people."

"Scared?" Elsie's eyes were on the photograph.

"I knew she was in it," Mary said. "I read the caption and figured it out. That's why you started spying on her, isn't it?"

"She hasn't changed much, has she?" murmured Elsie.

"No."

"The traitor," muttered Elsie.

"I wonder what happened to the baby," Mary said. "She never said she had a child."

"The liar. She thinks she's gotten away with it, too."

"You know how they cut off her hair at the hospital?" asked Mary. "She really does look like this picture, now."

"She is like this picture," said Elsie. "She hasn't changed. She was always the same, only we were fooled."

"I wasn't fooled," Mary countered.

"What do you mean? You were!"

"And I'm not fooled now," Mary went on. "Whatever this picture shows it's not the truth."

Elsie's head shot up. "Are you crazy? Look at her! She was a collaborator, probably even a spy. She slept with the enemy. She came over here to get away, to hide and start over like those Nazi war criminals in South America."

"I don't believe she was a traitor," Mary said.

"But here's the picture!" cried Elsie. "It shows her being one. It's history. She's in a book!"

"I don't believe it, anyway. I know Miss Fitch. She wouldn't do something like this. She was framed. Somebody made a mistake. It said so in the book, actually. Lots of people were accused of collaboration. Everybody was accusing everybody. It said that."

"But that's crazy!" shouted Elsie. "What about this baby you're staring straight at. Is it a doll? Maybe she was baby-sitting for the day."

Mary shrugged. "Maybe she was."

"And all those men who come to her house? What about them?"

"That's where *you're* crazy," replied Mary. "Miss Fitch isn't like that. And anyway, it has nothing to do with this picture."

"It has everything to do with this picture!" shouted

Elsie. She slumped on her desk and put her hands on her face.

"I thought you'd get it," she said through her hands. "I was sure you'd see when you looked at the photo. I was going to show it to you. I'd already decided."

Mary leaned over her. "Elsie?" she said softly.

"What!"

Mary squeezed into the desk chair beside her. Elsie even moved over to make room.

"The thing I don't get is you," Mary said. "You loved Miss Fitch. She was your friend. And she loved you. She thought you had talent, and guts. She would have done anything for you. You were special, her favorite."

"So what?"

"So, how can you do this to her? I think *you're* the traitor."

Elsie raised her head. "But I'm not doing anything to her," she answered in surprise. "She's the one who did things. All I did was find out."

"But, Elsie . . ."

"Listen. Miss Fitch knew she was no good right from the very beginning. That's why she came to this crumby town. That's why she lives here, four blocks away from us." Elsie clenched her fists.

"That's why she gives violin lessons to dumb kids like us who won't ever be any good, either. She knows we won't. Miss Fitch bottomed out in Millport, Connecticut. Only she didn't want to tell anyone, of course, so she put on this big performance. She showed everybody how great she was, and then she told everybody how great they were, to make sure they'd stay fooled. And they believed it! Too bad it was all a lie."

"But it wasn't!" cried Mary.

"Don't be so stupid."

"Well," Mary said, "I know how we can find out."

"How?"

"Let's ask her."

"Ask her!"

"Why not?"

"We can't ask her about something like this. How could we? What would we say? 'My dear Miss Fitch, we've found this ugly old picture of you. What on earth does it mean?' " Elsie mimicked a schoolteacher's voice. " 'And we've been noticing odd things going on in your house.' Oh, sure," said Elsie. "Ask her. She'd just lie her way out, anyway. She's been doing that for years."

Mary turned to look at her.

"It's only fair to ask her," she said. "What's not fair is to go around thinking things about her that may not be true."

"Except they are true," put in Elsie.

"Well, I'm going to find out," Mary said. "You keep on spying on her if you want to, and keep on collecting facts for your notebook. I'm just going to ask her, and whatever she says, I'll believe."

"Go ahead!" shouted Elsie. "I don't care. Do what you want!" She had risen from her desk. Her face burned.

"Go tell Mother, too! Tell the whole world. It's just what everybody needs to hear—how they all got fooled and get fooled every single day. How they can't believe anything, especially not what they see with their own eyes, because there's always some explanation, some reason. The whole world is mixed up that way. You can't put your foot down anywhere without there being a million reasons why you should put it somewhere else. And after that, a million more, until you don't know where to step next, until there's no place left to step!"

Elsie caught her breath and stopped. She was trembling.

Mary stared at her. "Elsie," she said, "you're scared of something, aren't you?"

"I am not!"

"What is it?"

"Nothing!"

"Are you afraid of Miss Fitch?"

"Of course not! Will you shut up?"

"Well, I'm not going to tell Mother," Mary said quietly, moving toward the door. "I'm going to go see Miss Fitch tomorrow, after school. I'll come home first, though, in case you change you mind."

"Oh, great," said Elsie. "Great!" She turned and flung herself into the chair.

12

About noon the following day, which was a Wednesday, the sky over Millport turned rat gray. By 3 P.M., snow was falling, the kind of small swirling flakes that bode large storms of evil intent.

Jimmy Dee, skulking on a bench outside the public library, saw it coming before anyone. Without a second thought, he headed over to the Millport Pizza Palace to stake out cover in a flanking alley. He knew from experience where the vents for the big ovens opened through the wall. He knew which corner caught the heat, which metal trash container retained it, which rotten eave of which rotten roof broke the down draft. He sat on a piece of packing crate, lit the end of a well-chewed cigar and watched the sky.

"Looks bad. Real bad," Mrs. Mott told Mrs. Cruikshank on the phone from her house. "I hear New York City is going to get hit right smack on the head."

"Serves it right," replied Mrs. Cruikshank. "Are you calling off our bridge game tomorrow?"

"Well, I can hardly see to the street already!"

Mrs. Mott hung up and went down to the cellar to hunt for the snow shovel.

In the kitchen of the Potter house, Mrs. Potter was taking stock of her food supplies, and groaning.

"Wouldn't you just know it?" she told Roo. "The very afternoon I was planning to go to market and here comes more snow. We've got spaghetti, I see. And these canned lima beans."

"Ugh," said Roo.

"A spring snow's the worst snow," Mrs. Potter went on, glancing out the window. "All those poor little animals just coming out to get warm; all the buds getting ready to grow, and then, snap, the freeze buckles them right down under again."

"This isn't spring," Roo pointed out. "This is just more freeze on top of freeze that was already there."

In her room at the top of the house, Granny Colie pulled down her shades. She turned her reading lamp up high. She took her sunglasses out of a drawer in the table next to her chair. Then she sat down to bask and wait for the arrival of tea. It felt just like Florida.

Mary came down the front stairs buttoning her coat. She tied a scarf around her neck.

"I'm going out," she called to her mother. "I'll be back for dinner."

"Out! But you've only just come in. And this snow!"

"It's not so bad. I've got to go see Miss Fitch," Mary called, louder than she needed for her voice to reach into the kitchen. She turned around and looked up the stairs. Nothing stirred. Down at the end of the hall, Elsie's door stayed firmly shut.

"Goodbye!" shouted Mary. But she stood before the hall mirror pulling her woolen cap this way and that. She put on her gloves, took one off again, inspected some loose stitching in one finger, then put it back on.

"I'm going now!" cried Mary toward the second floor.

Roo shot out of the kitchen wearing a white milk mustache.

"You've been saying that for ten minutes," she said, severely.

They went into the living room together. Mary sat on a chair and took off her gloves again. Heidi was there building something out of the furniture.

"What is it?" asked Roo, sidling up.

"A fort," answered Heidi. She had pulled a large blanket over the tops of two chairs to make a roof and blanket walls. Inside sat her beloved Paddington Bear wearing his blue coat and one yellow plastic boot.

"And you can't come in," Heidi told Roo. "See the sign?"

"Where?" asked Roo in a surprised voice.

"Here." Heidi pointed. "It says 'keep out.' If you can read, that is," Heidi added meanly.

"I can read," said Roo, who couldn't.

"Then you know what it says. It says 'keep out' and that means you."

"But Heidi! I want to come in!" Roo's voice rose anxiously. "Paddington is in there. I want to be, too!"

"You can't. You'd mess it up," declared Heidi. "I've got it all fixed and . . . and I'm doing my homework." She went inside the fort and dragged a flap of blanket over the door.

"You are not!" shrieked Roo, nobody's fool.

"I am!"

Mary put her gloves on for the third time and stood up.

"Heidi," she said. She walked over and stood, frowning, before the blanket. "Heidi. That isn't fair. You can't build a house in the middle of the living room and then tell people they can't come in."

"It's a fort," said Heidi from inside. "And yes I can."

"But the living room is everyone's room," Mary said. A prickle of anger was in her voice. "It's just plain mean to make a fort here. Look at Roo. She's all upset."

"I am not!" said Roo. "I don't even care."

"Yes, you do. You *do* care," Mary told her, angrily.

"I do not!"

"Heidi!" Mary was furious, suddenly. "Heidi! You are hurting Roo's feelings. Let her in, right now!"

"No!" yelled Heidi.

"Then, I'm coming in anyway!" Roo shrieked.

"No, you're not!"

"Then, I'm pulling this blanket off . . ."

"Wait, Roo!" cried Mary.

"And wrecking this fort!" screeched Roo. She gave

the blanket a mighty yank that toppled one of the chairs and collapsed the fort.

"You creep!"

"You dumbhead!"

Mary stamped her foot and turned to leav

"Mother!" wailed the little ones in unison.

Mary closed the front door hard behind her. Out-side, the snow fell thickly and peacefully. She tramped up the driveway toward the street, then stopped angrily to look back at the house. It was white with black shutters, as plain and ordinary as any on Grove Street. Who would guess from here what wars raged within?

Mary glanced at Elsie's windows, second floor, right corner. They stared back at her, pale, secretive, admitting nothing, asking nothing. There was no clue, at this distance, to who lived behind them. But even knowing who lived up there, even knowing her for fourteen years, didn't tell Mary anything.

"Talk about forts!" muttered Mary, and a new surge of fury went through her. "Who does she think she is, locking herself up like that? What is she trying to prove?"

Mary started walking. She lifted her chin and imagined Miss Fitch, lonely and hurt, in her small home up the street. She began to think of what she would tell her, gently, and of how surprised Miss Fitch would be.

"Elsie spying on *me*?" She would laugh at that. "Poor Elsie," she would say, and, "How sweet of you, Mary, to be worried." Mary smiled to herself.

"Hey! Wait up!" Mary spun on her heel in the snow.

"Wait!" Elsie ran to catch up, her coat flapping open. She wore neither mittens nor a hat. Mary glared at her.

"I thought you'd decided not to come," she said.

"Too bad, I'm here," said Elsie.

They walked in silence, reaching up to shield their faces from time to time. The sidewalk was slippery. The snow was beginning to mount up.

A little later Mary said:

"Well, what are we going to say, anyway?" But Elsie didn't answer, and they were, by this time, close enough to Miss Fitch's house to see it.

13

Miss Fitch could not sleep. Nine days she had been home from the hospital, and for nine nights her eyes had hardly closed.

"*Mon Dieu. Mon Dieu. J'arrive pas à dormir. Ah! J'arrive pas!*"

She caught herself muttering in French at odd times: after midnight, sitting up suddenly in bed, "*Mon Dieu!*" In the dark afternoons, alone with a book, "*Ah! J'arrive pas à dormir. Calme-toi. Calme-toi.*" ("Oh! I cannot sleep. Calm down. Be quiet.")

Why French after all these years? she asked herself. I speak English. I think *en anglais. Je suis* American. (I am an American!) But her mind was speaking French, babbling: *Mon Dieu! Calme-toi!*

It was the shock of the attack, she told herself. Of course. A great fright will send you back to your origins, to what you first knew and still know best. It was only the shock. She would get over it.

But she didn't. She got worse. She couldn't sleep.

White nights, she called them, from the French *nuits blanches* (sleepless nights). How appropriate! She understood the phrase all over again in translation. The blinding, burning wide-awake hours, the tossing on the hot, pale sheets had nothing to do with dark, with dreams. She was lit up live, sealed within a spotlight. Her eyes itched, then ached.

She couldn't read, couldn't listen to music. Naturally, she couldn't practice. Not with that arm. Her violin, a friend (a lover even!) through sadness and joy, through hope and disappointment all those difficult years, lay silent as a dead man inside its shut-up case. She became a wanderer in her own house, room to room, window to window. What did she expect to see? Out the front windows, the icy street carried cars and pedestrians by day: gleaming emptiness by night. Out the back, she watched the whitened garden, motionless except when wind passed through the bushes dislodging small clumps of snow.

She locked all the doors. Then: *Est-ce que je suis folle?* (Am I crazy?) She went through all the rooms and locked the windows, too. She drew the blinds tight. She was safe. She knew the number to call for emergency. She had visitors: neighbors and students. One evening she went to a concert, was thoughtfully driven to it by a student's mother. She had trouble driving her own car. The plaster arm got in the way.

She kept face. She made jokes about herself, all the old tricks from the past. "Sign here!" she told her visitors, handing them bright-colored felt-tip pens.

"Something scandalous! Something to shake up my old prune of a doctor." Her cast blared like a Broadway marquee.

Mon Dieu! Mon Dieu! She thought about things she had not thought about for a long time. They came, these memories, like the French words themselves, in a sort of babbling undertone, unexpectedly, up back stairways in her mind that she had closed off years before. She remembered a house, a street, a series of faces.

"Come now!" she snapped at herself. "Not that." The trouble was she had time on her hands. She was not yet up to teaching, the doctor said. (He looked exactly like a prune! All wrinkly and medicinal.)

"Give it a week or two. That head needs a rest," he told her.

Yes, and what a head. She was not eager to be seen looking so . . . so . . . crewcut. Like an American soldier. Like . . . like . . .

She knew what she looked like. Hadn't she been afraid of mirrors before? Hadn't she, then as now, wrapped kerchiefs around her head? She remembered. She did not have to look at herself to remember. The naked feel of her head on the pillow at night, the strange weight of that head (so light! too light!) sent her back automatically to other places. She did not want to be sent back. She fought to stay where she was. But the mind—ah! She rubbed her eyes and forehead.

The mind has ideas of its own, she thought. It makes its own connections. *Mon Dieu!*

She dressed most days, now. It gave her something to do. She was thinner than she had been for twenty years and fit into clothes she had worn during her concert touring days. Some of them were still pretty: a rose-colored skirt of fine, soft wool; a gypsy blouse with silk tassels. She found a chiffon scarf at the bottom of a trunk and flung it around her neck.

"Look at me! So slim. Young again." But that, too, brought the thoughts, the connections: a face, a sunny place in the forest, a picnic. *Mon Dieu!* She pushed the thought away.

She was about to unwrap the scarf, to put it back inside the trunk—and good riddance!—when the doorbell rang. Who? She rattled downstairs, opened the door (after glancing through the tiny peephole) to Mary and . . . Elsie!

"Good heavens! Two students of mine come to call in a blizzard. Did I forget? Did we arrange?" She patted her head in confusion.

"Oh, no," said Mary. "We just came. Should we have called? If we are interrupting we can come another time." She frowned a small frown.

"But, no! Not at all! Come in at once. You are more welcome than you know." She smiled at Elsie, that strange child. "Come in. Sit down!"

They floundered in, tracking up the hall with snow. Their heads and shoulders were quite white. Elsie's dark hair turned damp and clingy the moment it hit the heat. She wiped it back from her forehead and took off her coat. How long since she'd come there? Three months? Four? Miss Fitch could have kissed her.

"What a storm suddenly!" she cried instead.

"Yes." Mary removed her hat and hung it to dry with her coat on the coat rack Miss Fitch provided for her students in the hall.

"I was upstairs and did not notice. It is coming down quite hard now, I see."

"Yes."

"Are you warmer, now? Is it warm enough here?"

"Oh, fine. Yes!"

Elsie said nothing.

They sat in the living room facing each other. Miss Fitch's kerchief had fallen down over one ear. She reached a hand to adjust it, then smoothed out her skirt. She knew why they had come. She had known as soon as she'd seen Elsie, too proud and shy to come by herself. It was about resuming Elsie's lessons and, of course, their friendship. Miss Fitch understood such things. Her own life was full of sudden stops and equally sudden resumptions. People were so unpredictable, so human. They came and went from each other's lives, sometimes tiring of each other, then coming back together again. Miss Fitch had learned to wait, to accept. In the hospital, no. She had forgotten patience for a moment. She had written to Elsie a little desperately. She had missed her there, more than at home. A hospital will make anyone desperate. Elsie was not ready then. But, now, Miss Fitch gazed sympathetically at Elsie while her mind framed the words she would say:

"All musicians need a sabbatical—a vacation!—from

time to time. No questions asked. No apologies, no. Tell me nothing. I am only glad to have you back, my dear friend."

"We wanted to talk to you about something. There is something we wanted to know," Mary was saying, a little ominously under the circumstances, Miss Fitch thought. How dramatic these children were! So serious, they make it hard for themselves. Miss Fitch remembered that from her own youth. How a small thing, a tiny embarrassment, would churn and churn inside her until it turned big and catastrophic.

Now Miss Fitch turned her eyes to Elsie's cringing form and prepared to help her through this difficult moment. She raised her good arm and held it out to Elsie, and opened her mouth to begin. "My dear Elsie . . ."

Her hand was met halfway by a folded scrap of paper. It shot out of Elsie's pocket, between fingers which had twisted and kneaded it during the cold walk through the snow. It flew, thrust hard, to Miss Fitch's fingers. Mary gasped.

"You brought it?" she hissed.

Elsie said loudly: "We wanted to ask about this picture of you. We found it at the library." Then, she sat back on the couch and looked at her feet.

"What is it?" asked Miss Fitch, surprised. She unfolded the photo.

"*Mon Dieu!*"

Mary couldn't watch. This was not what she had intended.

"*Mon Dieu!*"

She had not meant to show the photograph, only to describe it in quiet words. That was the civilized way to do it. That was what her mother would have done.

"*Mon Dieu! Mon Dieu!*" Oh, my God. When Mary looked again, Miss Fitch's eyes were filled with tears.

14

"You must excuse me," said Miss Fitch, wiping her eyes. "I am so sorry." She brushed the tears back. Her makeup was smeared. "It is nothing, really. I am tired. I haven't been sleeping well."

Mary saw that she was fighting for control, and looked away.

"I had not realized there was such a picture," Miss Fitch said a minute later. The silence was awful. Both girls were struck dumb. Miss Fitch was not a person who wept. Mary's face was fiery. Elsie looked at the floor.

"Where was it?" Miss Fitch asked, after another minute had passed. "In a magazine?" She sounded more like herself.

"A book," mumbled Mary. "A picture book of the war. In the library. Elsie found it." It wasn't my idea, she wanted to add.

"Yes, I see. I haven't ever looked. Pardon." She went to the kitchen for a tissue, blew her nose and returned.

"Well! You must wonder what it is all about!" she said, trying for her old light-hearted voice. Elsie had her hard face back on again by this time.

"Yes," she answered coldly. "We wondered." That was too much for Mary.

"No!" she cried. "Not 'we.' 'You.' You wondered!" She turned to Miss Fitch. "Oh, Miss Fitch, I knew it wasn't true! I never believed it. I told Elsie it was a mistake. They made a lot of mistakes about people in the war. The book said so. I knew you wouldn't do something like this. Elsie believed it but not me. Not me!" Her hand chopped furiously in Elsie's direction.

There was a pause while Miss Fitch dabbed at her nose with another tissue. When she looked up again, it was to Elsie.

"But you are right," she said. "There is no mistake. This picture shows the truth."

"No!" shouted Mary.

"Yes."

Elsie folded her arms across her chest.

"What can I say?" Miss Fitch asked her. "There are things in one's life that one cannot explain."

"That isn't fair."

"Probably not."

"No," said Elsie. "I mean it isn't fair to pretend that you can't explain, to say things are not explainable. There are always reasons, good reasons and bad reasons. It's when someone does something for bad reasons that suddenly they can't explain."

"Elsie, stop it. That's horrible!" cried Mary.

Miss Fitch was staring at the photograph again. "This is why you stopped your lessons," she told Elsie.

"Wouldn't you?"

"And you couldn't come and tell me all this time?"

"Why should I? You were the one who wasn't telling."

"I understand," said Miss Fitch. "I would feel the same."

"No, you wouldn't. You're not like me. You never were!"

Miss Fitch nodded, as if this insult were perfectly acceptable. Mary couldn't believe it. Why didn't she get angry?

Miss Fitch was gazing at the photograph again.

"I was so young," she said. "Look at me. Just a child, really. Not much older than . . ."

"We are now," Elsie finished for her. "I know it. Don't you think I know? People always say that but it's no excuse. I'm old enough right now to know. It's no reason. Age doesn't matter."

"Yes, it does!" shrieked Mary, but no one answered.

"You can see things when you're older that you can't when you're young. You get wiser," she explained.

Nobody said a word. Mary felt silly, suddenly; childish and out of place.

Miss Fitch lifted her chin and spoke again:

"It is strange, this photograph. To see from the outside what I have remembered so long from the inside only. It was a small thing really, wasn't it?"

Elsie stared at her.

"Well, a cart, a crowd, some shouting—a little event, I see now. Afterward, the people, they went away to buy a vegetable in the market, or walked home to make a soup for lunch. They opened a shop for business or sat and drank a coffee in the café. Life went on for them. For me, yes, for a long time my life would not go on. It stopped just here, at this moment. Whatever I did, I did in the glare of this street. Whatever I said was drowned out by these voices. I went away, traveled, but the street followed. Oh, for a long time."

She stopped and smoothed the wrinkled face of the photograph.

"Now I see I must have escaped somewhere, in some place I can't recall. It is behind me now. I can look at this picture and see how far behind it is. Farther than I'd thought. Yes, I can think about it now. But can I talk about it?"

She seemed, really, to be asking for advice.

"Why not," said Elsie sarcastically. "Who's to know the difference. Mary won't tell. Everybody else has forgotten. What are you afraid of?"

"Of you."

"Me!"

"And of myself. Yes. Of both of us." Miss Fitch sighed. "Elsie, I am glad you have come. You can be angry. It is better so. You will help me think."

"And what about me!" cried Mary. "You keep forgetting. I'm the one who started this whole thing!"

"And Mary." Miss Fitch nodded absently. "You will both help me to think." But Mary could see that, for some incomprehensible reason, she was not the one who was helping. She was getting in the way, if anything, just as her violin lessons had gotten in the way, had wasted time that Miss Fitch might have spent more profitably with Elsie.

Out of sight, Mary's hand knotted to a fist in her lap.

Meanwhile, Miss Fitch thought. She pushed her kerchief back and forth on her head with little thrusts. Elsie watched her carefully. She took in every thrust, every flutter of movement on the older woman's face. She would have liked to spread her notebook on the table between them. A spoken word is a shifty thing, depending for its sense on the moment during which it is said. A day later, a year, and its meaning might have changed, reversed itself entirely to suit other circumstances.

Elsie's hand missed the weight of her heavy pen. She missed her desk too, so orderly and secure against confusion. By rights, Miss Fitch should have come to her room, she thought. There, Elsie could have listened and judged with a clear mind. Here, in Miss Fitch's foreign living room, who could be sure of anything? The air itself was thick with Miss Fitch's charm. Even the couch (Elsie was actually sitting on it!), the very same couch she had spied on through the window, was bewitched. Black and grotesque it had appeared to her from outside. Now, it seemed a rather quaint, rusty-brown old thing, worn out at the arms.

Elsie moved uneasily upon it. She felt trapped. When

she tried to sit up straight, the old cushions collapsed beneath her, drawing her down into a maddening slouch. Across from her, Miss Fitch had the advantage of a higher, hard-seated chair.

"It was a difficult time," Miss Fitch was saying, trying to bring up more excuses. "France was occupied, you see."

Elsie shrugged, but the couch smothered her shoulders. Her eyes were just level with Miss Fitch's throat. She raised her chin an extra, uncomfortable inch, and looked up at Miss Fitch's face.

15

When Miss Fitch opened her mouth to speak again, it was not to tell a story. Mary and Elsie knew the difference at once. A story has been told before and will be told again. Its words are worn with speaking, easy to say. A story has made a life for itself, apart from real life, perhaps even safe from it. Stradivarius's perfect ear, a dead fiddler's bad luck, these were stories. Miss Fitch's words were not easy to say. For forty years they had traveled with her, little bags of words packed away at the edge of her memory. For forty years they had remained unspoken, hidden even from herself.

Now she drew them out, reluctantly at first, warily, for they were words which still had power to harm her. She held them up for Mary and Elsie to see.

"I have never told this to anyone," she told them. "You are the first. In the beginning, there was the child to protect. After the child . . ." Miss Fitch smoothed the photograph. "After her, well, to be frank, I found it necessary to protect myself.

"People are vicious," Miss Fitch said. "It is a fact of life. They are afraid for themselves and therefore eager to condemn others. I had a life to live. Do you understand?"

"Yes!" cried Mary. Elsie said nothing.

"I have a life still," Miss Fitch warned Elsie, then waited for her nod.

"So, now we've made a bargain," Miss Fitch announced. Elsie frowned. She was aware that she had given something up, but could not quite see what it was.

"His name was Hans Loffler," Miss Fitch said quickly, as if she wished to get the name over and done with. "He was a soldier in the German army. The child is long dead," she added. "But this is not what you want to know. For that, I must start at the beginning."

And she began to tell about the war: about the German army marching headlong through Europe into France; about the fall of Paris, so quick and easy that it shocked the world; about the soldiers who came to rule over the people in Poland, in Holland, in Belgium and in France. Not only in Paris, but also in the smaller towns, the suburbs around Paris.

It was a strange scene she described, or it seemed strange to Mary, who could find nothing in that dark, terrorized past to compare with her own life in Millport.

Elsie, meanwhile, listened with a look of angry recognition on her face. Miss Fitch spoke of events which she knew well from her reading in the library. She spoke of governments fallen and countries disintegrated, of people confused, homeless, wandering. Elsie had imagined these fearful things already. She knew about that kind of fear. She had dreamed about it even and had felt it herself. Miss Fitch's words frightened Elsie just as the sight of Jimmy Dee slurping soup in her mother's own kitchen had frightened her, and filled her with fury.

"By what right did it happen!" she might have screamed at Miss Fitch. And: "You. You! It was people like you who made it happen!"

"The Germans came to my town," Miss Fitch explained, slowly, hesitantly. "They nailed posters to the walls of our buildings and shops. 'Trust us' these posters said. 'We come to help you.' The soldiers did not burn our homes or shoot us as we had feared. They were polite, orderly, but they took over everywhere. They moved into the houses of those who had fled. They took over the public buildings. They bought from our shops. In Paris, not far away, they attended our theaters and ate in our restaurants . . ." Here Miss Fitch faltered. Her hand clenched the tissue it held.

"Miss Fitch!" cried Mary. "Please! You don't have to tell us."

"No. It is all right. Elsie must hear this, and . . ." She smoothed the photograph gently. "This picture brings me back. The street here is my own. If you could see just here, around this corner, you would find my house. My father kept a small shop on the ground floor. He was a cobbler who repaired shoes and also made them to sell. Our family lived above, my mother, my older brother and I.

"When we heard that the Germans were coming,

we wanted to leave. Many people left. They packed what belongings they could and went away in wagons or cars. Everyone was afraid. We were afraid. But my father said: 'No. We will not leave. Where could we go? How could we live?' So, we stayed. Anyway, we had no wagon or car." Miss Fitch paused thoughtfully.

"I was fifteen, I think. Yes, fifteen. It was early summer. June, 1940. I was a student at a nearby school, and also, twice a week, I went by train to a small music school in Paris.

"I was very ambitious to play well, to have a great career. I remember that my father purchased for me a used violin. This violin and my lessons cost him more than he could afford, but I was wild for the music so he found the money somehow.

"I loved my violin and practiced very hard. But for some days after the Germans came, I did not dare to play. We drew the shutters of our house and stayed inside. We tried to be quiet. We were all afraid, even my brother. He was sixteen, too young to be a soldier and angry with our parents for not letting him go to fight anyway.

"At last, we were forced to come out to buy food, other things. Shops in the town began to open. People visited each other. My father opened his shop for business and life started up again, almost as it had been. Except, of course, everything was different. The German soldiers were there, watching us."

Elsie moved impatiently on the couch. "Look," she said, "I don't care about all this. Just tell what happened when . . ."

"I remember the first time a German soldier came to our shop." Miss Fitch's voice broke over Elsie's like a wave. She was picking up confidence, Mary saw.

"I had just come home from school and was upstairs with my mother. We heard the bell on the shop door ring and, then, a loud voice speaking very bad French to my father.

" 'Go look!' my mother whispered to me. I crept downstairs, quiet as a mouse. He was showing a boot to my father, pointing to a place where the sole had worn through and flapped open. My father nodded.

" 'Leave it here. Come back tomorrow,' my father said, rather loudly himself so that the German would understand.

"The soldier was very tall and he leaned over the counter looking down at my father. I had never thought of my father as a small man, but suddenly he looked small to me. His shoulders were small and weak. His face was worried and gentle. Too gentle, I thought. I went into the room and around the counter to stand beside him.

"The German was speaking again. At first, we could not understand him. His face turned red and his voice became louder. Then, we understood that he wanted his boot fixed immediately. Within the hour. This was not possible, I knew. My father could not work that fast. I was already shaking my head, beginning to explain, when I felt my father's hand on my shoulder.

" 'Come in an hour,' he told the German. 'It will be fixed.' When the soldier left, my father sat down right away to work on the boot.

" 'Always do what they say,' he told me, without looking up. 'Otherwise you ask for trouble.'

" 'But how will you finish?' I cried. In the end, we helped him, my mother and I. Like a nurse at an operating table, I stood beside him holding the proper tools, running to find what he needed.

"My brother was angry that night when he heard about the German coming to our shop, and about what my father had done.

" 'This is the enemy you are dealing with!' he shouted at my father. 'You are helping France's enemy when you fix his boot! Next time, you must refuse. Turn him out. Let him know his trade is not welcome in our shop.'

" 'Next time I will do exactly the same,' my father answered quietly. Of course, we all understood why my father had agreed to fix the boot, why he had to agree—because of us, his family. My brother was very angry, though. That evening, he was sullen and would talk to no one.

"After this, we often had German soldiers visit our shop. My father was a good cobbler. He could fix a boot so that it looked new again, and he charged reasonable prices. The word got around."

Miss Fitch shrugged.

"What could we do? Other shop owners had the same problem. Some people understood. But others in our town did not approve of my father's dealings with the Germans. Behind his back, they spoke against him, told tales that were not true. Women who had been my mother's friends turned their faces away when she spoke to them on the street.

"And at my school, I found that I had enemies for the first time. Before, of course, there were those who disliked me, whom I disliked. I was a reserved child, a little shy. Like you, Elsie, I did not have many close friends. This was different. Now I saw that I had real enemies, people who hated me. Not for anything I had done, oh, no! This was the hard thing. *I* was the same. They hated me because of my father, because their parents had spoken against my parents. It was frightening to realize suddenly that not only a schoolmate hated you but also his parents, his whole family. It made the hate big and serious, something that could never be fixed. One girl spat in my face.

" 'Pig!' she said, and spat. I was angry, but also ashamed and frightened.

" 'You don't know what you say!' I cried. 'These are lies you are believing!'

"She said, 'I know who is lying,' and walked away.

" 'Pay no attention,' my mother told me. 'That is a stupid family. All so proud and nose-in-the-air. The mother—did you know?—takes in other people's clothes for washing to make ends meet. Poor washerwoman, while her good-for-nothing husband spends the money to drink himself silly every Saturday night. They are jealous of us. Pay no attention.'

"My mother was a soft-spoken woman usually. Not a gossip at all. I had never heard her say such things about anyone. But I was glad to hear them now. To fight a whole family, you need a family behind you. I was glad to see my mother stand up and fight.

"Oh, it is strange to look back now and remember the anger of those days. Fear, yes. Everywhere fear. But beneath, hidden at the heart of the fear, there was anger. You would think, wouldn't you?, that it would have been enough to hate the Germans. And we did! Yes! We detested them, despised them, my mother, my father, everyone. We French are a proud people. To see the German soldiers strutting down our streets, smoking in our parks, eating at our cafés, it turned our stomachs. But who dared to speak of it openly? Who could protest?

"One small sign of protest, a wisp of a rumor, and the German eye fell upon you. Then, at night, some night when you least expected it, they would come with their guns to knock on your door. 'You are wanted for questioning,' they would say, most politely. 'It won't take long. Don't be afraid.' And that was that. Many who went away for questioning never came back.

"We heard it happen on our own street, my father, my mother, my brother and I. We heard the car drive up, and the voices, then the crying. We heard the doors of the car slam shut and we heard the car drive away. Next day, we would find out who, but never, almost never, why. We were terrified. Even my brother.

"But, deep inside, we were angry. And suspicious. Who had turned this man in? Who was the traitor? The Nazis were devils, but so great was our anger and our fear that we began to look for devils among ourselves. Every small disagreement, even petty incidents, took on large importance.

"If the butcher ran out of meat, you might easily convince yourself that he had sold it, for higher profit, to a German customer. Perhaps, even, he had made some arrangement with the enemy. Traitor! If someone acquired, from mysterious sources, a new winter coat that normally he could not afford to buy—there! He was suspected of collaboration. Rumors! Everywhere, suspicions and rumors. Some had foundation. Many did not. Do you see how it worked? Since we could not openly hate our real enemy, we turned our anger on ourselves."

Miss Fitch stopped, and looked across at Elsie, as if expecting her to say something.

"And the stranger thing was," she went on, "that we were all, in small ways, guilty of collaborating with the Germans. How could we help it? How could my father? They lived among us, conversed with us, devised the rules and regulations by which we were forced to live. We all compromised. We traded our pride for our lives, for the lives of our families."

Miss Fitch paused again, and shook her head.

"For us, it was a very bad exchange. I sometimes think that by the end of the war, we French had come to hate ourselves more even than we hated the Germans."

Elsie frowned. "But not everyone made that trade," she said. "I read about it. You didn't have to compromise. You could join the Resistance. You could fight secretly, make secret plans to blow things up. There were ways to fight!"

"Oh, yes," agreed Miss Fitch. "There were ways. I will tell you of one who chose to fight. Not a big fight. He was a small fish, a baby fish, who could not do very much to help. He was afraid, but he swallowed his fear and went to a meeting to make the very sort of plans you have just described. He crept out of the house late at night to go to these meetings, while his parents slept. They would not have let him go if they had known. They would have locked him in his room, tied him to his bed, anything to keep him away from those meetings. He was angry and headstrong, though. And very clever at climbing out of windows."

"Your brother!" whispered Mary.

"Gerard. Yes. He had not been at it very long when they arrested him.

" 'Poor Gerard,' someone told me later. 'He did nothing. Only came to listen, very serious, very straight in his chair. He ran some errands for us and then, poof! He was gone. It shook us up, I can tell you. But there were others, before and after him, who disappeared. It was to be expected.' "

Miss Fitch's voice trailed off. Her hand drifted up to her head, to the kerchief slipped cockeyed again.

"To be expected," she murmured, then looked at Elsie.

"Look at me!" Mary wanted to scream at her. "I'm the one who cares!" Miss Fitch sighed and looked at Elsie.

"That was the Resistance, you see. A few heroes and then, the others." Elsie's eyes snapped up.

"What happened to him?" she asked bluntly.

"Elsie!" cried Mary.

"He died . . ."

"Elsie! Will you stop this?" Mary was weeping, suddenly.

"He died in a concentration camp," Miss Fitch said.

"Elsie!" screamed Mary. Her eyes were flooded with tears.

"It's all right," said Miss Fitch. "It's the logical question to ask."

"No, it isn't!"

"We believe he died in a camp," Miss Fitch continued, to Elsie. "We believe he was sent to a work camp inside Germany. Many young men like him were sent to such places. My father tried to trace him, then and later. He could get no specific answers.

" 'Your son is safe,' he was told. 'No need to worry. He will write when he can. Be patient.'

"He never wrote. There was no word, ever. Only much later, we heard a story. How did it go? The older cousin of a boy who had known Gerard at school had a friend whose brother had escaped from a German camp. This friend's brother remembered a young man named Fichet at his camp. My mother was wild when she heard this news.

" 'You must find this person, this brother, and speak with him personally,' she told my father. 'It is the only chance.'

"Toward the end of the war, my father did contact him, by letter. Never in person. 'What did this Fichet boy look like?' he wrote. 'Can you tell us more about him?'

"The friend's brother was sick, in a French hospital, it turned out. Later we heard that he had died. He could not describe Gerard, if it was he, very well. 'What can I say?' he wrote back. 'We were all so dirty and sick. This person I knew only slightly, and I am not sure his name was Gerard. I am sorry.'

"As you see," Miss Fitch told Elsie, "we never knew exactly what happened. The times were chaotic. Communications were poor. In such disorder it was possible to lose people."

Elsie nodded. "Yes, I see," she answered.

When Mary looked up then, through her tears, through the clenched fists half shielding her face, she saw that Miss Fitch was smiling, a sad, gentle smile, at Elsie. And very faintly in Elsie's eyes, what was it? For a second, Mary thought she saw the flash of a smile reflected.

16

If Miss Fitch had caught Elsie's look, she gave no sign of it. She rose suddenly to turn on a lamp. The room had grown quite dark. In the hall, Miss Fitch flicked a switch that lit the porch light over the front door outside. She spread the curtains at a living room window and looked out. Now the girls could see the snow pelting slantwise across the window. Pelting, but making no sound at all. Subtracting sound, if anything, so that the clicks of Miss Fitch's high-heeled shoes across the hall floor, into the kitchen, stood out sharp and separate.

Miss Fitch turned on the kitchen lights and came back to sit down.

"Would you like something?" she asked. "Hot chocolate?"

"Go on," answered Elsie. The lamp light had turned her skin rosy. They all looked rosy. Mary's cheeks were glowing. Miss Fitch was still wearing the long, transparent scarf from the trunk upstairs. It glistened in the light, palest pink, magical.

She was magical, Mary decided, watching her. Straight and still, she sat in her chair, and her dark eyes gazed powerfully across the room, as if there were something there to be controlled or subdued by a force inside her. And if there was something there (Mary glanced quickly over her shoulder), if there was something no one but Miss Fitch could see, it *was* controlled, Mary was sure. Miss Fitch had strength. In the lamp light, she appeared stern, almost fierce. She was no victim, Mary realized suddenly. She was not some charity case to be sheltered and plied with soup and good intentions. She did not need Mary's sympathy, did not want her loyal heart. These were useless offerings, silly feelings that Miss Fitch rightly brushed aside because something more important was at stake, something to do with Elsie, and with Miss Fitch herself.

But what? Mary could not see it, and she was hurt. Angrily, she watched Elsie lean back on the couch, as if she knew this room well and felt a part of it. Angrily, she saw Miss Fitch lower her dark eyes to Elsie's face, and hold them there, full of strength and understanding.

"Well, go on!" Elsie's voice shot irritably through the room. Mary jumped.

Miss Fitch nodded. Her eyes were once more on the photograph.

"It's of no consequence, of course, but this picture, it is backwards," she said. "I have just noticed it."

"Backwards!" Elsie leaned forward in surprise.

"Printed in reverse, I mean. The street curves left here, not right. My family's house was around this corner, rather than that one." Miss Fitch pointed. "I remember clearly now. Everything here is backwards."

Elsie examined the photograph with a frown.

"Well, how could they have known?" she blurted out. "I mean, the people who made this book had obviously never been to your town. It looked like any old town to them." She sounded angry, as if Miss Fitch had accused her of making a mistake.

"No matter," said Miss Fitch. "I was trying only to put myself back there, as a girl walking along with my violin. I was a little arrogant in those days, I think." She glanced at Elsie, smiling.

"I worked so hard, you see. Nobody, I thought, worked so hard as I did. Privately, I thought very highly of myself and not so highly of other people, who were not so serious. I prided myself especially on my clear head. I knew what I wanted to do and how I would do it. I was very organized. I made a schedule and stuck to it." Mary looked over at Elsie. She was fiddling with a button on her blouse.

"That was before the Germans came," Miss Fitch said. "Afterward, well, it was impossible to have plans. My music school closed up. The teachers had gone away. A year later, it reopened, but by then the trains did not run to Paris. There was a fuel shortage. People rode bicycles, or walked. I had no money to buy a bicycle. It was too far, too dangerous, for me to walk.

"I practiced when I could at home. I was angry at

this war, frustrated all the time. It interrupted my life. I had planned everything around my violin, you see: my fame, great wealth, travel." Miss Fitch smiled at herself. "I could not imagine spending the rest of my life in that little town, among all those plain people. I wanted to get away, and then, even Paris was out of reach.

"Life became harder, too. We could not buy good food anymore as the war went on. There was no meat, no butter. Everything was rationed, even vegetables. And we were cold in winter. No coal, little wood to burn. And the war went on and on. There were those who thought that it would never stop, that life would be like this forever.

"We were very poor," said Miss Fitch, "and I was still growing. I grew out of my only coat. My arms hung out the sleeves and I could not fasten it around me very well. Too tight. Too small. You can imagine how I felt, proud, serious me, to be seen in such a coat. It is hard to think highly of someone who goes about like a scarecrow, hanging out of her clothes.

"I remember that I was wearing that coat the first day Hans came to our shop," Miss Fitch said. "I remember that it snowed. I came home late in the snow."

"Snow?" asked Mary.

"How strange," Elsie added softly, glancing toward the windows.

"Not so strange," Miss Fitch said. "Why strange?" she murmured. "Unusual, perhaps. Yes, and very beautiful that evening, a fine white veil of snow coming down over all our little town. I remember it so well. I remember . . ."

"Yes," whispered Mary. "I can imagine." And suddenly, she really could. She was forgetting her anger now, forgetting to be hurt. She was forgetting everything and becoming a part of Miss Fitch's story.

"I remember . . . I remember . . ."

Then Elsie was imagining it, too, for Miss Fitch had a way of speaking that lured people behind her words, even cautious people who have ever an eye on themselves.

Now, as Miss Fitch talked on, both Elsie and Mary saw clearly the person whom she was describing: a proud girl in a rough coat, standing on the sidewalk in the photograph. They could see her dig her fists into her pockets and hunch against the cold. They could see her bare legs, and the snow beginning to fall, thick and heavy, just as it was falling now, outside, on Grove Street.

Only, in Mary's and Elsie's imaginations, the snow fell on the roofs of the shops in the photograph; on the doorsteps of the houses; on the heads of the shoppers rushing to finish a day's meager marketing; on the shiny black boots of a German soldier who stepped, with menacing precision, up the sidewalk.

Was it then that the sound of Miss Fitch's voice faded in their ears? Later neither sister could remember exactly when Miss Fitch had swept them out of themselves into that other, wartime world. Later, Elsie did not like to admit that it had happened.

"I didn't forget to call Mother," she told Mary, after Mrs. Potter had phoned hours later to ask where on earth they were.

"And I didn't forget about the snowstorm, either," she sniffed. "I knew it was getting bad out there. I just didn't want to interrupt Miss Fitch."

But Elsie had forgotten, and Mary with her. They had forgotten because suddenly they were there, right there, in the photograph.

They stood in the street beside Renee Fichet and turned their faces to the sky to catch perfect snowflakes on their tongues. They rubbed their cold knees with their cold hands, as Renee rubbed hers. They watched a German soldier go by out of the corners of their eyes, and when he had passed, they walked with Renee up the street, around the corner, to a narrow two-story house where the front door rang a bell when it opened and a man glanced up from the shoe in his lap.

"You're late," he said. "Your mother is worried. Come in and lock the door. We'll have no more customers now the snow has started."

17

"Is that Renee?"

"Yes, Mama. It's me." She did not take off her coat, for the shop was cold. The little stove in the corner was unlit for lack of coal.

When she had locked the door, Renee put her hands into her pockets again and went to stand before the front window. Outside, snow fell into the darkening street. It was not a lasting snow. By next morning, it would be visible only as a raw dampness on roofs and sidewalks. Snow came infrequently to that small French town, and when it came it did not stay long. To Renee, now eighteen, it was enough of a rarity to stand still and watch.

"Look," she told her father. "It's so pretty. The windows are getting eyebrows."

But he did not look up. Outside, the hunched and bundled form of a woman passed by close to the window, and disappeared down the street.

"People are leaving tracks," Renee reported. "You

can see who has come in, who has gone out and not returned. M. Perrin has closed early, like us. I see his footprints going home."

M. Perrin ran a small bakery across the street. His home was elsewhere in town.

"But, of course, he has nothing to sell," answered her father briefly.

"Mme. DeGrelle's dog has been out," Renee said. She liked the street this way, the neatness of its shapes under the thin snowfall. She liked the tracks that told such clear stories of comings and goings.

"There," she said. "I see his little pawprints heading for the corner. Then, back they come, tip-tap. He didn't like this weather very much, I think."

Her father made no comment. Renee sent him an angry look. Even in good times it had not been his way to speak of small matters. Now, since Gerard had gone away (for this was how the family thought of it), since then, he found little to say on any subject. His thoughts were hidden, sealed somewhere back in his head. He did not appear angry or sad. He continued to repair his shoes with skill and patience. But he kept to himself, kept even his eyes down, or away, so that Renee could not talk to him without a sense that she was intruding.

Never, of course, did he speak directly of the war, or of the presence of the Germans. None of them did. Day by day, Renee's mother aired her bedding, shopped for food, chopped vegetables, washed clothes, with a weighty concentration that left no room for such talk. For her, it was enough to get through a day without trouble. Trouble was when M. Perrin ran out of bread before she reached the front of the line. Trouble was a hole in a pot that could not be repaired.

"What is happening to us? Why is this happening?" Renee might have asked. She wanted to know what to do about the war, what to think about it. After Gerard, she learned not to ask. Such questions brought only a shrug, a silence.

At night, in her cold bed, Renee heard her parents talk in their own bedroom. She heard the quick rumble of her father's voice and the higher tones of her mother's. She could not hear their words. What they spoke about, she never knew. Later, when she was older and the war was over and she had moved away, it seemed to Renee that from those nights dated her first bitter feelings of living separate, cut away from her parents. In their room, a magic circle of understanding, of explanation, closed around them. She imagined them asking each other questions that she was not allowed to ask, making answers she was not invited to hear. She lay alone in her bedroom, gazing up at the ceiling, and when she finally fell asleep it was because of loneliness that she fell, because there was nowhere else to go.

"Renee!" Her mother called again from upstairs, where a job waited. Renee turned, frowning, from the window. She was on her way across the room when, from outside, she heard footsteps approaching the shop door. The latch was lifted, then rattled. There followed a heavy knock.

"Look to see who it is," her father ordered.

"It's a German," whispered Renee, catching sight of a uniformed shoulder through the window.

M. Fichet put his work aside and stood up.

"Open," he told her uneasily.

The man who entered the shop a moment later was young, not much older than Renee herself, it seemed. He was no taller than her father, though his straight, stiff posture—or was it the stiff green uniform—gave an appearance of greater height. His hair was short, light brown; his face ruddy from the cold. His eyes darted at Renee, retreated with embarrassment, then settled on her father, who had moved over to stand behind the counter.

"Yes? What can I do for you?" M. Fichet said loudly. At the same time he motioned Renee away, upstairs. She took several steps toward the staircase and stopped. Suddenly, the German was feeling for something inside a pocket of his uniform jacket. She saw her father's eyes light with fear.

"What do you have there?" called M. Fichet. The young soldier stepped toward him.

"Please excuse me," he announced, "for intruding on you. Your shop is closed, I see, but . . ."

He drew from his pocket a squarish black object.

"It is my heel," the soldier said. He glanced nervously at the object. "It has, well, as you see, it has come off!"

Renee let go an audible sigh of relief. M. Fichet leaned on the counter.

"Let's have a look."

"I am sorry, really! It happened just now in the street. I did not even know it was loose." He spoke a heavily accented French. But it was accurate.

"Hand it here. Where is the boot?"

"But, I am in it!" said the soldier, full of confusion.

Renee suppressed an urge to laugh. They were not used to either confusion or apology from their German customers.

"You may sit there if you wish to take it off," said M. Fichet solemnly. He pointed to the room's only chair.

The soldier sat down and began, with a shy glance at Renee, to pull off his boot.

"Excuse me," he said again, addressing M. Fichet. His face was redder than ever now. "I am sorry, but perhaps you could help me pull? They have always been a little tight."

M. Fichet marched obediently around the counter to help, and after much twisting and yanking from either side, the soldier's foot was at last pried free. But when it came forth—what was that? Renee put her hand over her mouth to stifle a laugh. The young soldier's sock was riddled with holes, and at its front, a most unmilitary white toe poked through the flannel.

The soldier blushed crimson and hid the toe behind a leg of the chair.

"You are certainly in need of repair!" said Renee, unable now to keep from laughing. Her father frowned a warning at her.

"It is not me but the stupid supplies," muttered the

soldier. He looked like a small boy sitting there, self-consciously hiding his foot from Renee's eyes.

"The supply office has sent no socks. We are all this way. It is not just me!"

"Of course. The German army without socks. What a problem!"

A little grin twitched the soldier's mouth.

M. Fichet looked sharply at his daughter. "Renee, go upstairs. Quickly!"

But she didn't go. She didn't always, these days, do just what her parents told her. She sat on a stair and watched her father nail the heel back into place. And though she did not speak again, not even to say good-bye, it seemed to her that she could have said many things and that the soldier would not have minded. He was too young to mind, perhaps. Or too embarrassed. Or too nice. Yes, that was it, Renee decided, thinking everything over in her room that night. He was not like a soldier at all. She remembered his terrible sock, and smiled.

In the months that followed, Renee saw this soldier often about the town. He was a low-grade officer of some kind who ran errands for those of higher command.

"And what great job do you do in this war?" she asked him once, teasing again because he always looked so young and serious, a little like Gerard, she thought. Her father would have spoken to her angrily if he had heard. He would have warned her to be careful. She didn't care. She was tired of his warnings.

"Oh, not very much," Hans had answered. (She knew his name by this time.) "It is my French. They think I speak well."

"And do you?" she asked, passing him by on the street. Their conversation was never more than this, quick comments in passing. It was dangerous to be seen talking.

"You must know that better than I," he had answered, and marched straight on, with his eyes looking up the street.

She liked this. She liked: "They think I speak well." His answer seemed to put them together on a side against the others, against the stupid war itself.

"Have your socks come in yet?" Renee teased.

"Unfortunately, no."

"You must be in shreds by now."

"In blisters, you mean!"

He was certainly better looking than the other boys she knew. He held himself proudly, while they tended to slouch and scowl. ("But, of course," her father would have said. "His army has beaten our army.")

Spring came, then summer, the fourth summer of occupation. Renee's worn brown coat was packed away. She wore light skirts and blouses, never as pretty as she wished, not "in style," but clean, well ironed. A neighbor who was proficient at such things cut her hair in a becoming fashion.

She was not a schoolgirl anymore. She worked in her father's shop. She shopped for her mother. At night, she practiced her violin and dreamed of concerts, of her debut in a brilliant concert hall. She longed for peace, for release from the tension of watching, waiting, of never having enough. She didn't care what kind of peace it was. Any kind would do, just so the war would end and life could begin again. Any kind of life, anything different.

She looked out for him specially now, a matter of general interest, she told herself. His uniform looked different to her than those of other soldiers. He wore it differently, without arrogance. When other soldiers walked through town, they marched blind, careless of the people who scrambled aside to make way. Hans moved among the townfolk respectfully. He had charge of a truck, but did not race it down the street the way others did. He drove carefully, full of responsibility. Renee saw him stoop to pat the head of Mme. De-Grelle's stringy dog. She heard him speak quietly, though firmly, to a rowdy group of children playing in the street with a ball.

She thought he watched her, too. Stepping out of the shop for an errand, Renee's first thought was to see if he was there, if he had noticed. And when he did notice, she was pleased and walked faster, suddenly became more businesslike.

"I was in Paris for two days," he said one time. "I brought you something."

It was a piece of sheet music, a Schubert waltz.

"But, how did you know?" asked Renee.

"Play it tonight," he said. "I will walk past your house and listen."

She played it for an hour, nonstop.

"I love music," he told her afterward. "You play very well."

He was lonely himself, so far away from home. She saw it in his eyes, which lingered upon her for just an instant too long when they met. She had not thought of German soldiers being lonely before. She had not thought of them singly at all, but only as some monstrous wave that had swept over France, fastening it down tight with fear. Hans was not fearsome in the least. He seemed, if possible, rather frightened of her.

She began to wonder about his family, his mother, for he was certainly someone's son. She saw a letter poked out of his pocket, or was it a military document? She wasn't sure. Then, he came closer, and she identified the mark of the post. The thought that there were those who wrote to him, who cared enough about him to write, frightened her a little. For some days, he seemed too human, too real, and she did not look in his direction.

Perhaps he was hurt. A few days later came the note, which he delivered personally to her in the shop while her father's back was turned. (She liked this daring act from one who seemed so shy.) She did not respond at first. His written French was not as good as his spoken. It reminded her that he was German.

Then she answered, for no particular reason that she could think of. Perhaps it was boredom. Maybe it was to have a secret against her parents, against the whole world for that matter. She didn't know. She didn't care.

Later, when they had begun to meet secretly in the

little forest, when there was time to talk, she teased Hans about his bad spelling.

"I almost didn't answer your first note," she said. "A six year old might have done better."

"My mother learned French as a child," he told her. "She taught me to speak a little, but not how to write it down."

He talked about his family, about his two sisters at home, about his mother, a schoolteacher, about his father who was a farmer. He liked to tell about his home. He missed it badly. He disliked the army, he said. There was no one to talk to.

"I want to have a farm of my own," he told Renee. "A dairy farm would be best. I know a lot about cows."

He was shy to the end, serious, deferential. It was left to Renee to say out loud what as time went on they both felt together.

"It's so stupid, so crazy," she exclaimed. "Nobody wants to fight. Everybody wants to live. We are all on the same side really. Why are people so stupid that they can't see it?"

"I believe this, also," Hans assured her. "But what can you do? This is the real world."

The little forest was very beautiful that fall. It lay on land which had been owned by a rich farming family. They had gone away at the start of the war, to England, people said. So, the fields had turned to weeds and brush, and the woods behind the fields were open to whoever wished to go there. It was not a good place to walk. The trees were young and spindly, and bushes of all kinds grew among them. It was a good place to hide, to sit in one spot surrounded by vivid green walls, and to talk.

The most difficult part was getting to the woods, and then getting home again, without arousing suspicion. They knew the danger. Danger was in every person passed on the street, in every shape of a person across every field. German or French, it didn't matter which.

They came separately to the wood, with ready excuses. Mushrooms and berries to gather, for Renee. Suspicious movement around the empty farmhouse, for Hans. They knew they could be shot, or worse. They knew there were no excuses really for what they were doing. Once there, however, in the woods, privacy was so complete that all other worlds seemed to dissolve. Or so it was for Renee, who would lie on her back looking up at the wide, blue sky as if it were a window thrown open just for her. Hans sat nearby, planning out his farm. He built pastures and fences and little structures out of sticks.

"This is my barn," he explained with such childlike solemnity that Renee laughed. "And this, adjoining, will hold the tanks for milk," he continued, frowning at her. "I will have a very modern dairy and the cows will all be milked by machine. I've read about it. It can be done."

"So, is this what the army does? Reduces its soldiers to little boys playing with sticks?" Renee asked. "You need a vacation, I think."

"Laugh if you like, but I am quite serious," Hans answered. "I will do these things and must make plans. Here, hand me that branch over there and I'll show you my idea. Dairy farms can make money, these days. I don't intend to be a dull-brained farmer standing out in the sun with a rake. This is a business I'm talking about. We could make it work."

"We?" Renee asked, teasing.

"Yes, we," Hans replied, and the way he looked at her made her blush and smile.

They brought food and spread picnics between them. In Paris, Hans could buy little twists of good bread and sweets long since vanished from the local shops. He brought news, too, stories of disagreement, disarray among the German commanders; stories of incidents in Paris. They laughed about these over the food because here, in the wood, such things were properly distant.

"You are getting fat!" Renee teased, though he was as straight and lean as ever.

"And you. We must put some meat on your poor old bones," Hans said seriously, then laughed at himself because it was what his mother always said.

They did not begin to touch, to move close together, until the weather turned cool and closer seemed the natural direction to move. Hans was shy about this as well, so Renee took the lead.

"Is this real?" he asked once, looking into her eyes. "Do we really love each other?"

"Yes!" Renee answered fiercely. "This is real. It is the only thing that's real."

If the forest had been special before, now it became doubly so. It became a place to think about during the long boring hours of work, a place to dream about when all other dreams were dead.

"What will we do when winter comes?" Hans asked.

"Something," Renee said. "We'll think of something."

This was how they lived, day by day. It was how everyone lived during that war. But for Hans, winter never came.

Strangely, Renee could never remember later what they had talked about, what they had done, on their last day in the forest. She supposed it was because that day was no different from others which had preceded it. There had been a small picnic, probably; perhaps a letter from a friend in Germany for Hans to translate for her. ("At home, I have many good friends," he had told her. "You will like them.")

The afternoons had grown shorter and colder, she recalled. That day, the sun was already low in the sky when they walked from their hidden place toward the edge of the trees.

She was behind him, three yards or so, moving slowly in order not to break or bend the bushes. They were always careful not to leave trails which might point to where they met. They were careful, too, to separate at the woods' edge, to take different routes back to town.

"Everyone for himself," they had agreed, early on. Should one of them be detained, caught, the other must not feel an obligation to reveal himself.

Renee was walking behind Hans when she heard a series of twigs snap away to the left. She stopped, on guard. Hans walked on, hearing nothing, unaware that she was not following. Reassured by this, she was about to go on, to call, "Wait!" when up ahead bushes moved. Flew apart. Shots rang out—five, six, a clatter of gunshots that melted together in her ear to make a terrifying crash.

Renee saw Hans twist and fall backward, as if a powerful wind had blown him suddenly down. It happened so fast that she did not feel herself fall but found herself cowering on the ground, grasping clumps of weeds in her fists. Next came a period of time during which she did not think, did not hear, did not see. She lay clenched on the ground, a blind fist herself.

After a while, the woods moved around her again, and she was aware that she was alone. She saw that the sun had gone from the sky and that the forest had grown dim.

Renee rose to her knees. Waited. She got to her feet. She crept toward the place where Hans had fallen. The woods seemed empty now, but she was afraid of the dark places behind the bushes, and went slowly.

She reached the place and saw Hans lying face up on the ground. His eyes were closed, his head turned slightly to one side. A wound was there, underneath. She did not try to look at it or to touch him. She walked around him in a circle.

A little wind blew by her. It rustled the leaves and made her imagine footsteps in the forest. She crouched in brush and waited, but she was shaking badly now, and could not distinguish between noises.

Crouching, Renee watched Hans. His body covered more ground than she would have expected. He was like a giant fallen down over the little bushes, between the young trees. And like a giant, he made the place around him seem small and tight. She knew he was dead. The wind knew it, too. It played with him, flipping a bit of his hair back and forth over his forehead.

Renee felt the forest move in close around her. She felt the night coming down out of the sky. She heard the wind walking toward her through branches, and far off, she heard the sharp squeal of a rooster, or a human voice calling, she was not sure which.

She leapt up and ran. She left him there without thinking to cover him, without a tear or a backward look. She was too frightened to cry. She ran, and as she ran, the forest shut down, black and terrible behind her. It became an evil grove of trees, then a menacing mound in the field and finally a dark smudge fading away into the night.

Inside the smudge lay the uniformed corpse of a German soldier. Renee ran away from it. She ran back home.

18

Mary and Elsie were not aware that Miss Fitch's voice had stopped until they saw her rise from her chair. Then, in the new silence, they watched her walk slowly toward the living room's front windows. They saw her stand before the windows and cradle her cast arm in her good one. From there, they followed her gaze outside. They had followed her such a distance in the past two hours that they could not immediately detach themselves. Some part of Mary continued running with Renee in the dark. A portion of Elsie stayed behind to hover over Hans's body in the forest.

Outside the windows, a pale sheet of snow descended. This surprised them somewhat. They began to sit up, to straighten a blouse, rub an elbow, began to look around.

"What time is it?" Mary remembered to ask.

Elsie shook her head, still staring over Miss Fitch's shoulder at the snow. The shoulder turned suddenly, came about like a ship at sea, and brought the older woman's face to the light, so that every line, every hollow, was visible. Miss Fitch walked the length of the living room and stood before the windows at the opposite end.

"I have had the strangest feeling that I was being watched," she said.

"What?" Neither girl could tell for a moment if this was a continuation of the story or something real, now. Elsie stood up.

"Where?" she asked.

"No, not now. What a storm this is!" Miss Fitch turned again and came toward them. She put her good hand on the back of the chair she had been sitting in.

"Before," she said. "In recent days. Since the hospital."

"Watched by who?" asked Elsie.

"By nobody." Miss Fitch smiled reproachfully at herself. "It was no one, nothing, a trick my poor old head played on itself. I am fine now. Better than ever, in fact. Pull up the shades, turn on the lights, unlock the windows. You see? I am ready to come out again now."

"Out from where?" asked Mary, confused.

"From somewhere, who knows? From being afraid."

"Do you mean of that man who attacked you?" said Elsie.

"And him, too. Yes. Poor fellow. I see him clearly now. He was as frightened as I, and not right in the head, I think. 'Play, play,' he kept saying. I believe he wanted a concert in his honor."

"But didn't he beat you up?"

"He pushed me," said Miss Fitch. "Or lost his balance and stumbled. I don't know which. I fell. Then, bang, my head hit the table, and off I crawled to the phone. I was so dizzy I had to lie on the floor to talk. It wasn't pretty, no. I bled like a pig. Look here, I have ruined the carpet."

They followed her into the hall to stare at an ugly stain near the telephone.

"We heard you were attacked," said Elsie, a little resentfully.

"Attacked, yes. Attacked, no. Who cay say? I roll it around and try to decide. It was an incident. I will leave it there."

"An incident!" exclaimed Elsie.

The telephone began to ring, then, as they all stood around it. And there was Mrs. Potter asking, "Where on earth?" and reporting the lights gone out at the house, an electrical wire down somewhere up the street. Mr. Potter had hauled an old propane camp stove down from the attic and was attempting dinner, a combination of noodles spiced with lima beans. (In the background, Roo was in tears.)

"We are all right here," Miss Fitch told her. "Quite cozy, in fact. Can I keep the girls for dinner?" She glanced at Mary and Elsie and nodded. "And for the night? Yes?"

So, it was agreed. The weather was too treacherous for walking, some two feet of snow on the roads and they without their boots. It was no trouble. They could sleep in the guest room upstairs. And tomorrow?

"No school!" whispered Mary to Elsie, who was gazing fixedly at Miss Fitch, her hands on her hips.

They made dinner together in Miss Fitch's strange little kitchen, where nothing was where it should be (she kept the sugar in the refrigerator!), and not one morsel of food came from a can. They made veal in cream sauce seasoned with thyme. Mary snipped the thyme from a plant growing in a pot on the windowsill and chopped it fine with a sharp knife. They made a salad of soft lettuce and pieces of watercress.

"Watercress?" asked Mary.

"I found it at the supermarket," Miss Fitch replied proudly. "Imagine! Watercress in winter. They have everything there, truly everything!"

She showed them how to make a dressing in the bottom of a worn, wooden bowl: two dollops of vinegar, six of oil, a pinch of salt and mix fast with a wooden spoon.

"No pepper," Miss Fitch cautioned. "Pepper ruins a salad. Meat likes pepper, but not these gentle greens." She was in high spirits and tapped gaily about on her heels, just as if the forest outside of Paris had never existed, as if she had revived that grim memory only to pack it off and forget it again.

Mary rushed in her wake, smiling confusedly. Elsie watched with a serious expression on her face. She had a question to ask Miss Fitch, but she waited.

She waited until they had settled at the small dining room table, until Miss Fitch had praised the quality of the veal and applauded Mary's salad. She waited until they had sipped (Elsie raised her glass suspiciously) a first sip of the pale wine Miss Fitch poured into glasses from a tall, green bottle.

"What is it?" Mary asked, sounding so much like Elsie in her days of getting to know Miss Fitch that Elsie frowned at her.

"A specialty of the house," Miss Fitch said, smiling. "For tonight, to celebrate our lives, your short ones, my long one. And shall we prick our fingers, too, and run our blood together? I feel almost that we should!"

Miss Fitch laughed. She raised her glass high and looked through it. "It is a Rhine, a spatlese. A fine thing for a snowy night." Mary stared at her, uncomprehending.

"From Germany," Miss Fitch explained. "I have a case in the cellar."

Elsie set her glass down abruptly.

"Who did it?" she said. It was the question she had been waiting to ask.

"Who . . .?"

"Who shot him?" said Elsie. "You know, Hans. Who shot him in the forest?"

Mary glanced up, startled. "Elsie!" she would have cried, but she stopped herself in time. Across from her, Miss Fitch put her wine glass on the table and sighed. She looked at Elsie with dark eyes—with hurt eyes, Mary thought, but still she kept herself quiet, unwilling, this time, to interfere.

"I never knew," Miss Fitch replied. "I never asked."

"Why?"

"Because it was dangerous to ask. And because I didn't care. It didn't matter."

"I see. Because it was another one of these incidents," said Elsie. "Is that it?"

Miss Fitch glanced down. "In fact, yes."

"Why didn't they shoot you?"

"Perhaps they thought they had."

Elsie scowled. She was determined to have an answer.

"Was it the Resistance?"

"I don't know."

"Or it could have been Germans," Elsie went on. "Maybe they thought Hans was collaborating, telling secrets."

"Maybe."

"Or it could have been a person from your town, someone who knew you were meeting Hans in the forest, someone who'd been spying on you and was angry."

Miss Fitch shrugged. "Anyone," she answered tiredly. "It could have been anyone. You decide who it was. I don't care to think about it."

Still Elsie would not stop.

"Someone must have known what you were doing," she said, "because of what happened later, after the liberation."

"People did know."

"And when they saw you were pregnant, they knew why. And when you had your baby . . ."

"In July," Miss Fitch said softly. "The baby came in July. Yes, they knew. I don't know how."

"And then!" Elsie continued, almost triumphantly.

"Then, when the Germans were driven out, they came and got you."

But now, Mary could stand it no longer.

"Stop!" she shouted, and her fork fell with a clatter on her plate.

Elsie stared at it, surprised, her face gleaming in the candlelight. Mary picked up the fork and placed it carefully on the edge of her plate.

"Please stop," she told Elsie, quietly. "You don't need to make her say it. It's obvious what happened. It's plain as day. You must stop, now. Some people have feelings, you know."

Miss Fitch had spread her good hand over her eyes like a tent. Behind the hand, she nodded.

"Thank you, Mary," she said, so simply and kindly that Mary blushed. "It was enough," Miss Fitch said. "You are right. Quite enough." She lowered her hand and reached for the napkin to wipe her eyes.

"Now, I am all right again," she said after a minute. "Yes, thank you, I am fine."

She turned to Elsie.

"If you were asking if I was sorry, the answer is no," she said.

"I didn't mean . . ." Elsie began.

"I was frightened, though. Afterward, I went away to live in Paris with the baby. I was sorry for my parents. They could not go away. My mother was an old woman after the war. She walked slowly and thought slowly. My father took care of her. They were ashamed for what had happened. We did not speak openly. I was sick of everything, sick of them. The child was sick, too. She had a . . ."

Miss Fitch shook her head angrily. Her hand rose to her forehead to adjust the scarf.

"I was not sorry for that, either," she told Elsie. "In those days, nothing could make me sorry anymore. I picked up my life and went on. I was strong. I worked. I tried not to look back. Nothing is perfect in this world, I told myself. I am not perfect. They are not perfect. We contaminate each other. Let it be."

Miss Fitch glanced up at Elsie. "Or," she added sternly, "let it at least be understood."

Mary stared at her fork. And even Elsie did not dare to ask another question after this. She pushed her food into neat, orderly piles on her plate and ate careful mouthfuls. After dinner was finished, she was the one who ferried the plates to the kitchen and offered to wash the dishes.

"No, thank you," said Miss Fitch. "I never allow my guests to wash dishes."

"But we are not guests," replied Elsie, and she began defiantly to fill the old-fashioned sink with water.

19

The room that Mary and Elsie shared that night was as neat and plain as a room in a country inn. But a faint musty odor sprang from the twin beds.

"I don't know why I keep a guest room when I have so few visitors to make use of it," Miss Fitch remarked, showing them in. "I have thought of making it into a sewing room, but tonight, well, I am happy for it."

"What about all your friends?" asked Elsie casually. "Doesn't anybody ever stay?"

"My friends?" replied Miss Fitch. She gave Elsie a sharp look. "But, no. They do not stay here. They have their own apartments not far away. Most of them are boring old bachelors who need a well-cooked dinner, not a bed." Miss Fitch laughed at herself.

"So much the worse for me," she added, still laughing. "We elderly, single women have a poor time socially, I'm afraid." She took the blankets from the beds and prepared to make them up with clean sheets.

"Occasionally, I'll put up a traveler," she went on, while Mary and Elsie stuffed their pillows into cases. "My friend Gustav from France—have you met him? No? He was with me for a week last summer. He is a dear man, a violinist, like me, and lonely since his wife died four years ago. We all knew each other in the old days, touring. Well, and what do you think? He came all the way from Marseilles to court me. Yes! It is true. He asked me to marry him!

"So," said Miss Fitch. "So, you see, I am not completely in the pasture yet. I was quite pleased!"

"You turned him down?" Mary asked.

Miss Fitch laughed. "But of course, I am not a marriageable kind. And besides, he wanted me to come to live with him in Marseilles. Horrors!" She clapped a hand to her head to show her dread.

"He was here again this fall, one evening just after Thanksgiving. A sweet man, very lonely. I sent him away. 'Why me?' I cried, 'when you have thousands of beautiful French girls under your nose in Marseilles!' He will find someone soon. I will get a letter inviting me to the wedding. And perhaps, well, what do you think? Should I go?"

"I would," Elsie said, solemnly.

"It has been fifteen years since I was in France," Miss Fitch warned her. "Fifteen years since my father's funeral. What a long life he lived, and all in that little town. I would not go there, of course. But I could see Paris again. What do you think? Would it be good for me?"

"Yes," Elsie said. And then, with typical bluntness, she posed another of her logical questions:

"But do you have enough money for a trip like that?"

"Elsie!" shrieked Mary.

It was all right, though. Miss Fitch was laughing again.

"Elsie?" whispered Mary.

"What!"

They were in their beds, staring up at the ceiling of Miss Fitch's guest room. Mary rolled over toward her sister on an elbow.

"Aren't you going to say *anything*?"

"What should I say?"

"Well, Miss Fitch is no traitor, that's one sure thing."

"Who said so?"

"She did. That's what she spent this whole night telling us, remember? Didn't you *hear*?"

"I heard everything," answered Elsie, "including how she collaborated with a Nazi soldier . . ."

"She fell in love, you idiot!"

. . . and slept with him . . ."

"But she was so lonely. He was her only friend."

". . . and how she got him killed . . ."

"That wasn't her fault! It was the war. The war killed him! She was terrified."

". . . and then, how she lied about it and got caught. Got caught twice," Elsie said, grimly.

"She didn't lie!" hissed Mary, trying to keep her

voice a whisper. "She didn't tell anyone. That isn't lying. She was scared. She had to protect herself."

"It really depends," said Elsie, slowly, "on how you look at it." She put her hands behind her head and stared straight in front of her.

"And anyway," Elsie added. "Why do you care about Miss Fitch so much? She was never your friend."

Mary flushed under cover of the dark.

"I just happen to believe in her, that's all," she said. "I probably would have done the same thing in the war if I were her."

"No," Elsie answered thoughtfully. "No, I don't think you would. You never would have gone to the forest to meet Hans. You would have lasted through that war no matter how lonely you were. You wouldn't have betrayed your family and put them in danger, either. You care about other people too much."

"But I can imagine . . ." Mary said.

"But I might have," Elsie cut in. "I might have done all those things."

Mary was silent.

"It's scary, isn't it," whispered Elsie, "not knowing what you might do. Things get out of control, like in a war, and anything could happen. And not just in a war, but anywhere, anytime, things could get mixed up and go wrong."

"Yes," Mary said. "You're not the only one who worries about that."

"And then," Elsie went on, "everybody is there watching, ready to get you."

"Not everybody," Mary said.

"Just about. Miss Fitch wasn't the only one who felt she was being watched. I feel that way all the time."

"Elsie!" whispered Mary. "*You* were the one who was spying on Miss Fitch. You *make* people into enemies. You cut them off and don't talk to them and keep secret notes that nobody is allowed to see."

"Untrue," said Elsie. "I'm just watching out for myself."

"Like Miss Fitch was protecting herself, right?"

Elsie didn't answer.

"Only, you're really not like Miss Fitch at all," Mary said. "She's like me. She believes in her friends. She trusts them. And," Mary added proudly, "after today, she knows I'm a friend. Maybe I can't play the violin as well as you do, but I'm her friend. She needs me."

"Oh boy," said Elsie. "One 'thank you' from Miss Fitch and you're off and running. She doesn't make friends as easily as you think. She guards herself."

"Well, at least she knows I'm on her side." Mary looked across at Elsie's dim shape in the dark. "At least she knows I won't tell on her."

"Who said I was going to tell on her?" asked Elsie.

"Or spy on her."

Elsie leaned toward Mary. "If you ever tell Miss Fitch about that, I'll kill you!"

"Don't worry," Mary answered. "I wouldn't tell. You still don't get it, do you? I wouldn't tell even if you weren't going to kill me."

"I know." Elsie leaned back on her pillow again. She stared at the ceiling. "I guess I wasn't planning to kill you anyway."

After this, there seemed nothing left to say. Both girls lay in their beds thinking, privately and sleepily, just as they used to do, years before, sharing a bedroom that was too small, in a house that was too noisy, on a street that watched and whispered and gradually fell asleep, too, in spite of itself.

Meanwhile, outside Miss Fitch's house, the snow fell slowly, then more slowly, then ceased. It covered the roofs and dormers along Grove Street, giving the houses there the very same eye-browed look that Renee Fichet had noticed so long ago on her own street. It whitened the corroded chain-link fences surrounding the downtown factory buildings and dignified the shapes of the ramshackle warehouses.

Over at the Millport Pizza Palace, Jimmy Dee brushed snow off his coat and stood up to stretch his legs. He was cold and a little stiff, but otherwise unharmed. He was thinking of another place, a safer and happier place that he would rather have been in. When the sun rose warm in a clear blue sky the following morning, he was still thinking of that place. He kept it in his mind all afternoon and into evening, when he ate, very respectably, a potluck supper in the basement of a good-natured church. And that was something for Jimmy Dee—to remember a thing for so long.

As the sun went down that next day, he could be seen mounting a street that led up from downtown to the residential areas. He looked as disreputable as ever in his baggy coat, but his mind was clear and full of music.

20

The snow melted quickly. After all, it was nearly April now, and spring must come sometime. Along the fence in front of the Potters' house, small heads of crocuses could be seen: purple, yellow, lavender. They didn't wait for the drifts to melt. They grew presumptuously through the snow, and bloomed.

"Crocuses are independent plants," Mrs. Potter told Heidi and Roo. "They come and go as they please. They don't like to wait on the weather."

"Like Elsie," Roo said. Heidi giggled.

They were out in the yard together for a sniff of fresh air, all wearing their winter coats. Mrs. Potter was pushing the last of the drifts away from the fragile blooms. It was an act of charity that pleased her.

"There!" she said, straightening up at the end of the row. "Doesn't that look better?"

"Let's go in," said Heidi. "I'm freezing."

"And I must cut the cheese and make a dip," Mrs.

Potter remembered. "What time is it? Good heavens! They'll be here in an hour."

They trooped up the back steps into the kitchen.

"Who's coming to your party?" asked Roo, when she had unzipped her jacket.

"Everybody!" sang out Mrs. Potter proudly. "Everybody on the street who knows Miss Fitch, and all her students, and all their parents. I invited everyone I could think of, and mostly everyone accepted. They didn't mind at all that it's so last minute. And Miss Fitch is coming, of course."

"Can I pass the hors d'oeuvres?" asked Heidi.

"Yes, you may, and put on something pretty because Miss Fitch will be watching you."

"She will?"

"She's going to see if you're ready for violin lessons yet. We've been talking about it."

"Who says I *want* violin lessons?" demanded Heidi. "Why does every person in this house have to play a violin? I want to play soccer."

"Soccer!" said Mrs. Potter.

"On the town team. You can try out if you're eight. I asked."

"I want to play soccer, too!" shrieked Roo.

"You're too little," declared Heidi. "And, by the way, your stupid blocks are all over my side of the room. I can't even breathe in there with all your . . ."

"Well, all your dresses are hanging up in *my* closet!" Roo cut in.

"Those aren't my dresses anymore. They're yours! Mother put them there."

"I don't care. I don't want them. If you want me to pick up my blocks, you'll have to take out those dresses first."

"But I didn't put them there!"

"So what?"

"Mother!"

"I want to pass hors d' oeuvres, too!" screeched Roo.

"Mother!"

But Mrs. Potter had her head in the refrigerator.

"Soccer!" she was muttering to herself.

Miss Fitch was the first to arrive, fittingly, for she was the guest of honor. She came in a blaze of finery, in red silk and perfume and the highest of high-heeled shoes. Around her head was wrapped, with fascinating twists, a silvery scarf, and long, silver earrings hung from her ears and her eyelids were molten with silver. Her cast was hidden discreetly beneath a shawl.

She was beautiful, radiant, and did not look at all like a person who "needed cheering up" as Mrs. Potter had said when she told Mary and Elsie about her idea for the party. Miss Fitch swept into the cluttered Potter living room as if she were a bird just flown in from Paradise. She shook Roo's little fist with solemn dignity. She accepted a potato chip from Heidi and plunged it obediently into the dripping bowl of onion-soup-mix dip. She exclaimed over a pair of dusty figurines on the mantel and asked to see where "the girls" practiced their music: "Good light is so important!" she announced.

Next, Mary and Elsie came down from upstairs, rather shy in their party dresses. (For it seemed so odd to have Miss Fitch there. Would she notice the discolored patch on the rug? Did she care about the burnt-bread smell rolling out of the kitchen?)

"Oh! My little toasts!" cried Mrs. Potter, springing across the hall for the oven.

Miss Fitch turned to Elsie.

"Dear one," she said, and kissed her on the cheek. "But, how fine you smell!" she added, smiling. "Is it perfume? Yes? You are dressed to perfection!"

"We tried just a little of Mother's cologne," put in Mary, who was standing a bit to one side.

"And Mary!" Miss Fitch wrapped her around with a hug. "My defender! My warm and steady one. You look grown up today. It can happen to a girl in a moment, don't you think? I remember it myself: one minute I was little—no bigger than Heidi over there—and the next, *voilà!* I looked into my mirror and a young woman looked back!"

Elsie gave a snort and stared at the floor.

"Oh, it's probably just this dress," murmured Mary, her cheeks flaming.

"Well, perhaps I've forgotten," said Miss Fitch in a voice that told she had forgotten nothing. "Perhaps there is more to it than looking into a mirror. Nevertheless, I congratulate you. Both of you! You are visions to behold."

The other guests began to come, then. In twos and threes, they were escorted by Roo into the living room, and relieved of their coats and pushed firmly toward

Miss Fitch. Not that they needed pushing. (This was Roo's idea of hospitality.) Everyone was pleased to see Miss Fitch. Everyone loved her. What a reputation she had made for herself in Millport. And which student was it that had got into Juilliard last year?

"Nobody yet," Miss Fitch replied sweetly. "But I have some promising ones coming up." She glanced meaningfully at Elsie, but as Mrs. Mott had just arrived in a mountainous white fur coat that blocked everyone's view, there was some question whether Elsie received the message.

Yes, they were all there. Mrs. Cruikshank was heaving satisfied sighs over having gotten inside, at last, the disgraceful house that Mrs. Mott had talked about for so long.

"It doesn't look so bad in here as I thought it would," she whispered to Mrs. Mott under cover of the chatter. "I guess they cleaned up for company."

Mrs. Cornelle had her eagle-beagle eyes out for drunks, drug addicts and escaped convicts. Alas! Everybody looked quite respectable.

"Silver eye shadow!" she tittered to Mrs. Landsbury. "Imagine!"

"Does Miss Fitch come from New York City, too?" asked Mrs. Landsbury.

"And where's your better half?" mewed Mrs. Mott when Mrs. Potter came by with a tray of sardines on toast.

"Traveling, I'm afraid," said Mrs. Potter. "This came up so quickly we didn't have time to plan around him."

"Well, it's a fine party. Such a pleasant idea after all Miss Fitch has been through. She looks pretty good for someone who just stepped out of a hospital bed. How long did you say she'd been home. Two weeks?"

"Yes, and have you met my mother, who lives with us?" said Mrs. Potter. She had just caught sight of Granny Colie standing hesitantly at the crowd's edge in her bedroom slippers.

"Indeed!" exclaimed Mrs. Mott. "She lives *here*?"

"Mother!" called Mrs. Potter. "Over here!" She lowered the sardines to a table and went to fetch her.

"Very pleased to meet you," Mrs. Mott intoned suspiciously, for Granny Colie had not seen fit to dress, and was in fact wearing her most venerable bathrobe.

Granny Colie eyed Mrs. Mott from head to foot.

"Do I *know* this woman?" she inquired presently.

"No, I was just about to introduce you. This is . . ."

"Then, I'd rather not!" snapped Granny, and she turned her back and shuffled off toward the kitchen.

Behind their tall glasses of fruit punch, Mary and Elsie glanced at each other and smiled. They were standing together in front of the fireplace. Really, there was nowhere else to stand. The crowding was terrible.

"Somehow, Granny always knows what's up," whispered Elsie. "Just when you think she's off in outer space for good—bingo!—she zeros in for the kill."

"Did you see what she ordered Mother to get her last week?" asked Mary.

"What?"

"One of those headphones that plugs into radios. She listens to rock music up in her room at night. She says it keeps her blood moving."

"That's not a bad idea."

"It's a great idea," said Mary. "But they're expensive. You have to get the radio, too."

"Have you got any money?"

"A little."

Elsie rattled the ice in her glass.

"Actually," she said, as if it were a small matter, "actually, I've been thinking of selling my desk set."

"You have?"

"Well, it takes up a lot of space on my desk. Who needs a stamp box, for instance? And the pen is so big. It's really not made for writing, more for signing things."

"But it's so beautiful!"

"I guess so. I'll have to think about it."

A whoop of laughter erupted suddenly from across the room, and the girls looked up to see Miss Fitch in the middle of a throng of guests. She was telling a story, and from the reproachful look on her face, it seemed the joke was, as usual, on her. It was part of her charm, this ability to tell on herself. Mary sighed deeply.

"She's more beautiful than ever," she told Elsie. "I guess she's well again."

"Or she's got herself made up to look that way."

"You know," said Mary. "Miss Fitch *is* a fraud in some ways."

"I know," Elsie said.

"I mean, how can she just cover up everything that happened to her during the war? How can she get all dressed up and pretend there isn't one dark thought in her head? Where do all those feelings go?"

"I don't know."

"And she came to America to get away," Mary said. "I'm sure that's part of it."

"Yes, it is."

"And maybe she even has lovers."

"She's an actress, all right," said Elsie. "Look at her. There's probably a whole lot of other stuff we don't even know, that we'll never find out."

"Like why she came to Millport at all. This is a strange place for someone like her."

"And why she's sitting around teaching violin if she's so good, supposedly. Why she stopped performing herself."

"I never thought of that," said Mary.

"She's a mystery," remarked Elsie. "One of those people who, the closer you get, the more you can't figure them out."

Mary glanced at her sister. "Like somebody else I know," she said softly.

"And maybe you don't want to figure them out," Elsie went on. "Maybe there are better things to do than worry about it."

"Maybe." Mary gulped the last of her punch and caught sight of her mother across the room. She was juggling a tray of cheese in one hand and a box of crackers in the other.

"Help!" she cried to her daughters. She nodded

violently in the direction of the kitchen, where another cloud of black smoke hung just inside the door.

"It's the cheese puffs," Elsie said stoically. "I knew they'd never make it."

"I'll get them!" cried Mary.

"No, I'll go," Elsie said. "I've had about enough of this, anyway." And off she went with her chin held high and her small, determined shoulders slicing through the crowd.

21

Spring was well underway before Jimmy Dee heard the music again. The daffodils beneath the tree in Miss Fitch's front yard bloomed and faded. The tree itself—a crab apple—produced a cloud of pink flowers, shed them, then thickened with leaves. The air turned warm. Birds sang feverishly from the bushes in the long evenings.

In back of Miss Fitch's house, Jimmy Dee's own laurel grove grew rich with blossom. On the branches, thousands of white florets opened out like tiny parasols, each printed inside with a miniature design. He was fascinated, and flattered, by such beauty from a place that had provided only shelter before. The bushes bloomed for him, he thought. He was a little shy before them, as if they offered too much, and dared pick only one floret each visit. This he mounted, stirred by some memory of elegance, in the top buttonhole of his ragged coat.

Meanwhile, he waited for Miss Fitch to play again,

all patience, during many nights. He saw her make supper and wash up. He saw her move about her living room, sometimes quiet and thoughtful, sometimes rushed with energy. He sniffed the flowers. They had an earthy odor, not like some he'd smelled. In the dark, they glowed. He felt himself glowing, too, but dimly, full of patience.

In the beginning, when he first discovered that Miss Fitch was home again, Jimmy Dee had felt afraid. Not afraid that anyone would catch him there. No. With Miss Fitch came the return of his old sense of safety, of having found at last a place unassailable by the outside world. He was afraid of himself, afraid that he would feel again the twisty thing in his chest that before had sent him loping across the yard, galloping insanely toward her back door.

"Play! Play!" he had screamed, and put his frozen hands on her shoulders to shake her.

Now that she was back, he remembered everything. He forced himself to remember, and went over the details in his head. The trouble was, his head was not always clear. Out of fright, he drank less, guarded himself in the laurel bushes. It wasn't so hard. He talked himself into patience and picked a single floret for his buttonhole. He could wait for years, he thought, but saw as well that it wouldn't be that long.

She was as eager as he to start her music again. Her students had already reappeared. She taught them majestically in the afternoons. Her old floating movements had returned. In the evenings, she opened the case that held her violin and brought it out to polish. She kept books of music open on the music stand, and read them, brow furrowed, like a minister at the pulpit.

Jimmy Dee knew what a cast was. He'd had some of his own in his time. He put his left hand on his right sleeve and imagined the texture of plaster there, hard and stiff. He recalled the supple lines of her arms when she played. He understood. And waited, ringed by flowers.

One evening, Jimmy Dee arrived late, long after dark. He had spent the afternoon on a bench in the weedy park across from the library. He had sat in the sun, and later, because the day was warm, he had pulled his long legs off the ground, laid his head on his arm and gone to sleep. He made a hopeless picture lying there, a dirty hump of a man, with one boot falling off for lack of laces. Passersby went around him with space to spare. Mothers called their staring children back closer to the swings.

He slept all afternoon undisturbed, which was unusual. Perhaps the police officer who patrolled the area from a car had been called to another part of town. He slept into the evening. Waking finally at about nine o'clock, he was fortunate to find an almost untouched peanut butter sandwich in a trash can by the park gates going out. He rewrapped it gingerly in its wax paper and shoved it in his pocket. Then he began, in the dark, the slow journey up the hill toward Miss Fitch's house.

Jimmy Dee did not hear the music until he rounded the side of the house into the back yard. Certainly, it would have been better if he had sensed it first as a strain in the wind, and then, coming closer, had heard a distant melody. He should have been allowed, after waiting so long, to creep up to it slowly, to control its force by his own approach.

As it was, the music hit Jimmy Dee square on the head when he rounded, in his usual hunch, the corner of Miss Fitch's house. A window had been left open back there. The sound of the violin rushed through, driving straight into Jimmy Dee, knocking him backward as if it had substance.

He keeled over heavily on the grass and put his hands on his ears. He pounded his ears with his fists. He staggered to his feet, glanced instinctively over his shoulder, and ran, crouched low, to his laurels.

From there, he hardly dared to look. The music surrounded him. It came from all sides at once, louder than he had ever heard it, buzzing and boiling. He tore at his ears and peeped timidly toward the house.

She was there, playing, just inside the windows. She played furiously, her whole body stretching, dipping, as if the violin had hold of her rather than she of it. Her fingers ran crazily along the neck, faster and faster. Her bow arm plunged and soared, plunged and bucked, but at the center her face—he saw it in profile—was still, perfectly concentrated.

Miss Fitch reached the climax of her piece, and slowed. Her fingers tread more gently on the strings.

Her bow gave out a fine ribbon of sound that curled and rolled over itself, repeated a phrase and then stopped. Her forehead glistened. She mopped it on a sleeve of her blouse, still grasping the bow.

The next thing that Jimmy Dee heard was clapping. This noise came from inside the house, also, but from farther back, beyond Miss Fitch. From the shadow at the side of the room it came, light, steady clapping. Jimmy Dee leaned forward in surprise, and as he did, a small figure stood up from behind a chair. It was a girl, he saw, dark-headed and thin. She walked toward Miss Fitch, still clapping, and the older woman laughed at this and raised her arm with a flourish to brush some loose strands of hair from her eyes.

Jimmy Dee had never thought to clap before. Now, amazed, he saw it was the right thing to do. He brought his palms together softly at first, then louder and louder, until the laurels shook around him and the air was full of clapping. Inside the house, Miss Fitch bowed grandly, a sweeping, crowd-pleasing curtsy. Jimmy Dee knew it was for him, and for a moment, yes, he was tempted. His foot even moved a fraction of an inch toward the house. But, at the last minute, he drew back into the bushes again.

Jimmy Dee knew magic when he saw it. One touch and poof! She might vanish again. He wasn't about to risk that. Jimmy Dee leaned back on his bush and when Elsie stopped clapping, he did, too. He was already waiting for the next piece of music to begin.